Spain's duc
R.E. Dos

Spain's duchess

R.E. Dossett

Copyright

 ISBN: 978-0-244-66454-1.

1

During the summer solstice of 1799, the noblemen in the Kingdom of New Galicia held a ball in their capital, Guadalajara. Many Spanish American noblemen, from the Viceroyalty of New Spain as well as the Viceroyalty of New Grenada attended this feast. It was the last year of the 18th century and many of the attendees were of good cheer for the coming century. Many were still wondering if the Spanish Empire would survive the challenges that would emerge in the coming century. Some thought that the Spanish Empire would dissolve after warfare with its neighbours, others even considered the fact that Spain might collapse due to the size of its empire – encompassing four continents. Few of the attendees did not want to bother that much with the question whether their empire would survive coming century.

At the ball, there were many peninsulares – Spaniards born on the Iberian Peninsula – present. Those peninsulares were invited by the New Galician noblemen who wanted to preserve New Galicia's prestige position in the Spanish Empire. There were also Spanish officers and even politicians that were sent, by Spanish ministries, to inspect the well-functioning of the autonomous New Galicia. The ball was held in a French style, with masquerade dancing, classical music, and an extended banquet. At the ball, there were two French diplomats present who were observing the informal politics on behalf of the French embassy that was seated in Mexico City. Those two French diplomats, Jules, and Floris noticed that there was animosity between the pro-Bourbon and the pro-France attendees. The pro-Bourbon attendees agreed completely with the policies of Charles IV. The pro-France attendees, or the Francophiles, longed to reform the Spanish Empire after the values of the French revolutions – with a more liberal government managing the Spanish territories, instead of the Iberian aristocracy which were kept in check by the Spanish institutions (such as the military).

After the ball, on the 5th of July, news was published in Spanish newspapers throughout the Viceroyalty of New Spain that two politicians – from the Iberian Peninsula – were murdered in Guadalajara during the midsummer ball: 32-year-old *Felipe Victoria y Gazzette* and 22-year-old *Filemon de Montana y Valdes*. The bodies of the two men were examined by forensics after they were discovered in a brook near the Royal Palace – which was inhabited by the royal governors of New

Galicia. On the 10th of July, the bodies were placed on a ship towards Cadiz, Spain – with a note to the relatives of the victims. The Viceroy even decided to pay for the funeral expenses to ease the shock of what happened. For months, it was a big mystery what happened to the two peninsulares that were in New Spain on an inspection on behalf of the Ministry of War.

Late September 1799, a farmer from the Province of Oaxaca confessed that he participated in the transportation of the body of the two murdered politicians on June the 23rd of that same year. The Oaxacan farmer received a small compensation of 100 Spanish Real and debt relief from his landlord, who was involved in the conspiracy. After this confession, the Spanish authorities arrested the landlord of this Oaxacan farmer – a 29-year-old *Luis de Aragon y Valdes*, who recently inherited large plots of land for his deceased father *Calvin de Aragon y Playas*. Luis was released after just one week of detention due to his minimum role in the whole matter: He only provided the transporter of the corpses, after being blackmailed by several gang-stalkers. Even though the interview with Luis did not bring forth much information, there were two names that came out of Luis' mouth several times: Gregorio and Fiona Rodrigues.

Fiona Francisca Rodrigues y de Olmeda (1781-1875), the daughter of *Gregorio Amadeo Rodrigues y Camões* (1751-1823), was elected to President of a foundation that looked after disadvantaged Mayans in the Provinces of Chiapas and San Salvador. The foundation received its funds from twenty-two wealthy landlords throughout New Spain. The foundation was the initiative of a mestizo veteran that returned to his hometown, Chimaltenango, in late 1789. As part of the Bourbon Reforms, some of the Mayan towns became disadvantages and local economic recessions followed the early 1790s. In 1793, on the 13th of October, the foundation was established in Guatemala City and twenty-three donors signed up for its sponsorship. The foundation managed to alleviate poverty in many of the remote villages that were located at the Pacific Ocean. Fiona became the President at age eighteen, and just ten days after the sixth anniversary of the foundation. Her term was supposed to exist for eight months until the next *Praeses* would be elected. She has been living in Guatemala City since she was sixteen. She was born on a farm, near Guayaquil, as the daughter of Duke Amadeo II, who inherited a big estate from his father, Duke Amadeo I, who in turn inherited the estate from his grandfather Duke Carlos, the

first duke of the territory. The family estate consisted out of four extended farms, three villages, and two artificial lakes. The inhabitants in the Dukedom were around three thousand people. Fiona's father was permitted to carry the title duke by the Spanish Crown. The Bourbon Reforms did not cost him anything. Amadeo II only had one child, Fiona. His wife became barren after the birth of their daughter. Amadeo II joined a military club in the Kingdom of New Galicia, one of the main territories of the Viceroyalty of New Spain.
The mentioning of Amadeo II and his daughter, Fiona, caused the Spanish authorities to look deeper into Gregorio's reputation as well as his finances. Several detectives, hired by the Royal Audiencia of Quito, found out that Amadeo II had a reputation of extorting various shop-owners throughout Quito. He was also a sworn enemy of the Alvaréz cartel that controlled most of Quito's economy – at the expense of the smaller noble and rich households. Even though the detectives in both Mexico City as well as San Francisco de Quito could not find a motif for Amadeo II's alleged crime, he became their prime suspect. Because the double homicide concerned politicians form the Iberian Peninsula, the Spanish military took charge of the investigation instead of the regular criminal courts.
Currently, Fiona lived in the Captaincy General of Guatemala and she maintained some correspondence with her parents who lived near Guayaquil. She also maintained some correspondence with some relatives in Spain. She hoped to visit the Iberian Peninsula soon.
On the 25th of October Fiona held a speech at a convention in San Pedro de Matagalpa (also shortened as Matagalpa), Province of Nicaragua. It was her first main speech as the President of the foundation. She was proud that the event went well. She wore a long purple dress at the event in Matagalpa, while her fellow staff-members wore modest clothes. She wanted to get attention and be seen. She got what she wanted. All the guys in town began talking about her and she even walked around in that purple dress days afterwards (to be recognised). Her staff considered her behaviour excessive and improper. Some even considered her dress to provocative. However, everyone kept their mouth shut out of respect for her position. Some of the attendees of the event even became a bit uncomfortable when she spoke in a seductive manner to the public.
Four days later, on the 29th of October, Fiona and her staff were at a small coffee house drinking chocolate. This time she wore a yellow

dress that ended between her groin and her knees, together with white sandals with thin golden straps. She also wore a yellow straw hat, a feminine design, with colourful Mayan decorations at the band of the hat. She also wore a dream catcher as a necklace as well as two silver rings on her left hand.
'Well, that went well!'
'Sure', one of the staff members pointed at her dress, 'if you go around like that, you surely get attention!'
'This is just for promotion.'
'Promoting your body, you mean?'
'Come on, guys. This is nothing bad.'
'Well, you were convincing though!'
'When I gave my speech, I could see the eyes of the crowd. Those people were stunned by my speech and by my looks. As a result, all of them donated large sums of money to the foundation.'
'How much have we gained?'
'Well…', Fiona checked her notes, '4.400 Spanish Real!'
'Wow...'
'Fiona, we never gained so many donations.'
'Yes, it is mostly between 100 and 400 Spanish Real.'
'Well,', she felt satisfaction with the result, 'due to me gained tenfold this time!'
'Where is our next event?'
'Hold on', the event-planner checked his agenda, 'Santa Ana…'
'The Province of San Salvador!'
'Who ever visited that place?'
'I did… It is a lovely place!'
'I am curious to visit it!', Fiona checked on the map, 'It is close to the capital!'
Fiona looked around. The coffee a bit crowded with older people.
'I think we should come back to this place somewhere in the future.'
'I do not even think we need any more events after all the money we gained today!'
'We will continue to do events', Fiona said sternly, 'that is what we are appointed to do.'
'We know, boss… we know.'
'We can have party's though!'
'YEAH!'

At that moment, a group of five young men entered the coffee house. The five young man, aged between sixteen and twenty, worked in a nearby tavern. The five men drank some black coffee while discussing some of the rude customers they received past month. The five tavern employees were Samuel, Andreas, Fernando, Randy and Rensy. The men have been working at the tavern for two years by now.
'You know… the boss really should kick those rude people out!'
'I agree, Andreas…'
'But… guys… we depend on such loud and nosy customers. They are the ones paying most of the money!'
'Still… it is not healthy to be somewhere and to be treated like trash.'
'In that case, we would need to find another job.'
'Rensy… you got an official warning, right?'
'Indeed… next strike and I am out.'
'Ouch!'
'Well, I do not mind.'
'Do you have other work.'
'Not yet…'
'Be careful.'
'Do not say that', he finished his black coffee, 'The boss has to be careful! If he fires me for some dumb bullshit, I will beat his ass.'
'Then you will spend several nights in jail.'
'And he will have to recover months from his wounds… so I still get out better than he does!'
'You need to renew your mind man.'
'That type of thinking, Rensy, will get you in prison or even the death penalty.'
'Yeah man… you need to control your temper a bit more.'
'Temper…'
'Do not be in denial. This character flaw of yours is an open door for Satan to rob you of all that is dear to you.'
'Let Satan try… I will be waiting for him!'
The others laughed at his arrogant statement.
Fernando looked around and he saw a group of young people, five men and four girls, sitting at a table in the corner. One of the girls, wore a yellow dress and she sat with legs crossed looking around the coffee house.
'Guys… who are those people in that corner?'
The others looked in the corner. Samuel recognised them.

'That is the council of the Santa Barbara Foundation in Guatemala City. They support marginalised Mayans and other natives.'
'Hmm… who is the one in that yellow dress?'
'She seems like a harlot…'
'Her name is Fiona Rodrigues', Andreas informed them using a pamphlet he found in town, 'She is the President of the Santa Barbara Foundation… She is the daughter of the Duke of Amatique.'
'Amatique?'
'Not the District of Amatique here in Guatemala. There is a tiny district, in South America, also called Amatique…'
'I thought so…'
'So, she is the daughter of a duke… that makes her the future duchess.'
'She can already call herself a duchess.'
'What is she doing in Matagalpa? This is not a prestigious place at all.'
'She is not the one deciding the agenda of the foundation.'
'Well, whoever did that made a mistake.'
'I heard that the foundation received many donations here…'
'People around here do not care much about disadvantaged Mayans…'
'Well… they do care about a sexy lady asking for cash.'
'True to that…'
'Then the duchess played it smart.'
'Why are they still around here?'
'Maybe they have another even nearby.'
Rensy suddenly made eye-contact with Fiona and Fiona smiled at him. He became aroused and he felt the strong urge to make a chat with her.
'Guys… I am going to the bathroom.'
'Rensy… do not shit all over the place.'
They all laughed.
'Later…'
After completing his business in the bathroom, he washed his hands with flower soap at the sink and he went outside to smoke a tiny cigar. While he was smoking, one of Fiona's male staff members joined him.
'Can you light my cigar, please?'
Rensy lit the man's cigar.
'Thank you!'
'You are from around here?'
'Nah', he blew out the smoke, 'I am from San Pedro Sula.'
'Hmm… I am from Leon.'

'I like this province… it is incredibly quiet compared to where I am from.'
'You are here for work?'
'Yes', he spit on the ground, 'did you attend the benefit concert five days ago?'
'I did not…'
'You missed out man. There were various musicians performing good music… Good foot… hot ladies… and my boss, the president of this foundation, gave a speech and she sang a song afterwards.'
'Is your boss here?'
'She is the one in that yellow dress.'
'Ah… her?'
'She is hot, is she not?'
'She is!'
'What are you doing here?'
'I work at the San Antonio Tavern nearby… we are on a break now.'
'Hmm… we considered staying at the San Antonio Tavern, but we considered it too expensive. So… we chose the guesthouse across the street.'
'Ah… I see.'
'We will head towards Leon tomorrow morning… we will attend some party and from there… we return to the capital.'
'That is a long trip!'
'Guatemala has good infrastructure. That is one thing the Spanish do well!'
'Your boss…'
'You want to come and say hi?'
'Ehmmm….'
'Come with me!'
The male staff member returned inside with Rensy.
'Hey guys… this is Rensy. Rensy… we are the foundation looking after deprived Mayans.'
'Hello…'
Everyone greeted Rensy and Rensy sat down on the opposite side of the table, facing Fiona. After short introductions, everyone received another beverage – this time a pineapple beverage that was popular in The Philippines. Rensy also got one drink on the costs of the foundation.
Meanwhile, Rensy's friends looked at him sitting with the foundation.
'He is smart…'

'Going to the bathroom.'
'Just an excuse to get close to them.'
'What does he want from them?'
'They are a foundation that got a lot of money… maybe he wants some of that fresh cash.'
'He is nuts!'
'Let us wait and see if he books success!'
'He really wants to get rid of this life here.'
'Can you blame him? I do not want to do low paying jobs forever…'
'Well… we will see!'
The foundation staff decided it was time to go. Fiona chose to remain behind and Rensy also stayed at the table.
'So… you work in a tavern?'
'Yes, ma'am.'
'Just call me Fiona. I am just eighteen!'
'I am nineteen!'
'Great… we are of similar age then!', she ordered a tiny coffee, 'where do you live?'
'My home is just a two hundred meters away from here. It is a tiny cacao farm belonging to my grandfather. We are not that well off, that is why I work jobs.'
'Be glad you can work for your own money.'
'What?'
'Some people think that having money dumped into your bosom is a blessing. I am telling you; it is not! Why do you think I decided to work instead of wasting my breath in idleness?'
'Hmm… you are from South America, right?'
'I was born in the Kingdom of Quito, belonging to New Grenada. My dad is a well-off exporter.'
'So why are you in Guatemala?'
'My father is a member of some prestigious club in New Galicia, so he often travels between the two kingdoms.'
'From the Pacific Coast that is quite easy, right?'
'It is… there are less pirates over there.'
'True', he smiled, 'the Caribbean is haunted by robbers!'
'I would like to sail in the Caribbean once.'
'You must be out of your mind.'
'Then… that might be the case. I want it anyway. It would be so exciting!'

'So, you are leaving with your staff?'
'Tomorrow morning. First Leon and then back to Guatemala City. It is going to be a long ride.'
'Three days to Guatemala City?'
'Or four… depending on the quality of the horses.'
'The Spanish breed fast horses… so that will not be a problem.'
'I hope you are right… when we cam here it took five days because one of the horses collapsed in San Miguel… so we had to hire new ones.'
'Oh dear…'
'We were almost late for the event. Fortunately, we departed two days too early.'
'Better early than too late.'
'Indeed!'
'What is your full name?'
'Fiona Francisca Rodrigues y Olmeda… you?'
'*Rensy Emanuel Sanchéz y Estevéz.*'
'Emanuel… I like that name.'
'It means: God with us.'
'What are you doing tonight?'
'I have no plans… probably finishing some chores at the tavern and then playing some football with the guys.'
'Spend the evening with me. I could use some fresh company.'
He was overwhelmed by her request.
'I take that as a yes. Silence is consent!'
'Where?'
'At the public library. On the second floor. Be at 19:00 precise.'
'I will!'
She stood up and she left. Rensy also went outside to smoke another tiny cigar. His friends joined him.
'So… what was that about, Romeo?'
'Me? I was invited by one of those staff members to meet them.'
'You sat with them for twenty minutes.'
'They were chit-chatting all the time.'
'What is your plan?'
'Plan? I just wanted to see if there is some opportunity for me to leave this place.'
'I do not blame you!'
The area of Matagalpa was surrounded by hostile Matagalpa-Indians who lived in tiny villages where Spanish people were not welcome.

From time to time, Matagalpa gangs would raid Spanish goods in the city or on the roads. For this reason, the Captain General requested five hundred extra troops from Spain to defend the area against Matagalpa gangs. The Matagalpa gangs were also unwanted by the locals who wanted to preserve their urban life in Spanish society.
Rensy was mugged four times by Matagalpa chiefs, at one point he was even tortured because he was mistaken for one of their targets. Since that incident, two years ago, his opinion of the Matagalpa gangs became worse: He wanted them gone from Guatemala FOR GOOD! His uncle was murdered by a Matagalpa gang when he refused to bend over to their claims. Rensy was strongly motivated to leave the area.
'So… let us go back to the tavern. We have some work to do!'
That later afternoon, Rensy completed his work properly and quickly. He wanted to be off the job as soon as possible. When he finished his work, he checked out at his employer.
The employer, a French migrant who married a Matagalpa woman, grabbed him at his shoulder.
'Monsieur?'
'Rensy… I need to talk to you! It is urgent!'
'I am here', he turned around, 'what is going on?'
'I got threats lately.'
'From whom?'
'Chieftain Justo…'
Chieftain Justo was one of the main chieftains around. He was in rivalry with the other eight chieftains. The Matagalpa gangs did NOT get along. Chieftain Justo was the most violent of them all and he was also involved in the dark arts.
'What happened?'
'He wants your head!'
'Oh shit…'
'Rensy… you are good boy. I was always fund of your straightforwardness and your realistic attitude. I cannot afford to endanger my guest by having you here, but I also do not want to fire you. But I must choose my battles wisely, also because I have a wife and five daughters that depend upon me. I need to let you go!'
'I understand, Sir!'
'Wait…'
The employer came back with a bag with money.

'It is 100 Spanish dollars', he pushed the bag in his right hand, 'RENSY! I do not want to see you in this town again. This place is not safe for you. I have a bad feeling that soon someone will stab you or shoot you. For your own life's safe, GET OUT OF THIS PLACE!'
'I will!'
Rensy left with the money. He walked towards his grandfather's farm where he entered his tiny room. He did not want to tell his grandfather that he was fired and that his life was likely in danger. He did not want to involve his grandfather in this mess. He was glad that his employer fired him and even handed him money to move on. He remembered the appointment he had with Fiona within one and a half hour. He went downstairs and he saw that his grandmother-in-law made some dinner. He ate and he returned to his room. He packed some stuff in a bag, including the money he received from his employer, and he left.
While walking through town, he looked around him continuously. He did not want to be gunned down nor stabbed suddenly. He did not want to become paranoid. He realised that he should have left town a long time ago. This was not the first time that people advised him to leave Matagalpa. He walked towards the public library where he waited across the streets.
He never went to the public library. Reading books was just not his thing. He preferred to be outside, working, playing, and exercising.
Just ten minutes before the appointed time, he saw Fiona passing by – in the same outfit she wore earlier that afternoon. Instead of greeting her, he just followed her into the library. She went to the receptionist, where she handed over two Spanish dollars.
'Miss Rodrigues. Here is your key. You can hand in back tomorrow morning.'
'I will probably hand it in earlier.'
'Good! My colleague will be here from midnight on!'
'¡Gracias!'
She walked to the second floor, where she opened a small conference room. The conference room had one desk, two bookshelves, a small sofa, two paintings on the wall, a map of the Kingdom of Guatemala and a soft table in the centre. She sat on the sofa, which was imported from the United States. The conference room was often used by local businessmen who had to discuss contracts as well as conflicts with local farmers. The conference room had a large window, covered by green curtains. She picked some rum from the desk, two small glasses, and

some incense. She ignited the incense, and the room was filled with a lovely smell. She sat down, leaning towards the wall (with a pillow behind her back), while pouring rum in the two glasses on the table next to her. When she finished pouring in the rum, Rensy walked in.
'I am here.'
'Good! Right on time!'
'I always am!'
'Sit down', he sat next to her, 'Drink some!'
'I had no idea you liked rum.'
'I like a lot of stuff…'
'Why the library?'
She drank all the rum in just several seconds. Her speed shocked Rensy.
'It is quieter here than in the guesthouse where I am at.'
'Fair enough…'
'How was work?'
'I got fired.'
'What?!'
'The boss got threats… because of me… so he gave me some money and he told me to leave town.'
'Who is after you?'
'Justo Rojas is how people call him. He is a Matagalpa chieftain who opposes Spanish rule. He is the biggest menace to the Spanish here in Nicaragua.'
'Why is he after you?'
'Two years ago, I was mugged again in town. This time I fought back. Nobody blamed me. There was this girl, a year older than me, who lied on me that I raped her.'
'She did…', Fiona felt anger boiling when she heard that, 'what?'
'She made a false rape accusation about me. I was not even around when it happened. However, this was the excuse that Chieftain Justo used to target me.'
'You are the scapegoat.'
'Kind off!'
'What will you do now?'
'I am leaving.'
'Where?'
'I do not know… anyway, as long as it is away from here.'
'You can join us to Guatemala City if you want.'
'Hmm… that would be nice. I can work at your foundation too.'

She suddenly kissed him on the lips and grabbed his chest. He was overwhelmed.
'I got a better idea!'
She rapidly took off her panties and began kissing him again.
That same moment, five armed thugs arrived in the street where the library was located. The five men were sent by Chieftain Justo to kidnap and kill Rensy. What Rensy was not aware off was that two of the agents of the criminal chieftain saw Rensy at the coffee house chatting with Fiona. The two followed Fiona afterwards towards the guesthouse where she lodged. Those two swiftly informed their chief about what they saw. Chieftain Justo appointed three more men to them and the five were sent out with the mission.
One of the men rode on a mule, following Fiona towards the library. That man did not see Rensy standing across the street – because Rensy put on different clothes after leaving his grandfather's farm. It was a wise decision of Rensy to change his clothes, or else he might have been gunned down before entering the library.
The five men walked around in the streets. The civilians got suspicious and one of them rushed to the nearest Spanish garrison about the matter. The Spanish garrison immediately send thirty-armed cavalry troops to the street. When the Spanish troops arrived, the five thugs opened fire on the soldiers. The civilians panicked and everyone ran away from the street. The people in the nearest streets heard the gunfight and they also saw the people fleeing. The commotion was big. Two of the thugs died on the spot and the other three were arrested by the Spanish troops. One of the thugs confessed immediately that they were looking for Rensy Sanchéz.
'Where were you supposed to find him?'
'He was with a tall European woman, brunette, wearing a yellow party dress.'
'Where?'
'At the library, Sir!'
The one in charge of the cavalry signed two officers to come to him.
'Enter this library and investigate whether Rensy is here. He is likely accompanied by a foreigner. Arrest both once you find them.'
'Yes, Sir!'
The two soldiers even got help from the library's staff in finding the two. The receptionist did not note down that Fiona hired one of the small conference rooms. His intuition warned him not to do that. While

the rest of the staff joined the soldiers in looking for Fiona, the receptionist quickly walked towards the room that Fiona hired. When he arrived in the hall, he heard some loud feminine moans. He also sensed some strong incense burning. He walked towards the door, which hidden in a corner, between many bookshelves. The door was not closed properly. While he stood there, the two Spanish soldiers suddenly passed by. He distracted them by telling them that he saw a couple leaving the building. After the soldiers, and the staff, rushed downstairs, he carefully closed the door.

Fiona was riding on top of her new lover, when he unloaded his white liquid into her womb. Neither Fiona nor Rensy heard the door closing nor did they even noticed any of the commotion outside. The two were distracted by their natural lusts for one another. After Rensy had his spasm, Fiona stood up and walked towards the window. This was when she first noticed that there was some commotion outside. She had no idea what the crowd was shouting about. She put her yellow dress on, her hat and her jewellery. Rensy was completely exhausted. She opened the window and she saw various cavalry troops marching around in an empty street.

'Rensy…'

'Hmmm?'

'Come and look at this…'

'Hold on', the young man slowly rose, and he walked towards the window, putting his hand on her waist, 'What is it?'

'You are naked… put your shirt on before anyone sees you!'

'Who will see me on the second floor at the window…'

He put on his short and he returned to Fiona's side. She kissed him.

'What is this about?'

'I wish I knew, Rens…'

Rensy examined the whole situation and he realised that something quite bad just occurred. When he looked down, he could see two corpses and he recognised one of those men.

'You see that man lying there', he pointed in the right direction, 'he was someone that mugged me two years ago.'

'Has he been following you?'

'I do not know…'

Fiona suddenly felt intense danger in her intestines. She knew that this was a warning sign that they had to leave.

'I feel quite bad, Rensy.'

Rensy was not that well with paying attention to his intuition. However, this time he knew that they had to leave the library undetected.
'We leave, now!'
Rensy put his clothes on, and he put his arm around Fiona's waist, and he guided her through the library.
'How are we going to get out of here?'
'Just follow me lead, darling.'
Rensy led her to the backdoor where both escaped. The two walked, hand in hand, through an alley until they reached the coffee house. The weather was quite warm, even though the clouds became greyer with the minute.
'It is going to rain soon.'
'Hmm.... I need to get back at the guesthouse.'
'I will bring you.'
'Where will you stay?'
'I will stay with you!'
At that moment, the Jules and Floris received updates about the situation in the Republic of France. The reports revealed that Napoleon Bonaparte's campaign in Syria and Egypt were a big failure and France was still at war with the Habsburg Dynasty that controlled the Archduchy of Austria.
'Oh my God… when is this Napoleon going away?'
'I am not sure he is ever going away, Jules.'
'Well… I just hope he does not become the next consul.'
'If he becomes consul, the whole revolution of ten years ago would have been for nothing.'
'We can better focus on what is going on here in Spanish America.'
'Did you find out anything about that Spanish duke?'
'Gregorio Rodrigues? He is in Quito as usual. He has not set foot in New Spain since the solstice ball. He has a daughter who lives in Guatemala.'
'Why is she there?'
'She is the head of a foundation', he showed his partner a newspaper, 'she is heralded as a smart woman.'
'Where in Guatemala is, she?'
'At the moment, she is in the Province of Nicaragua at the charity event. Well, the event happened last week.'
'Then she is likely there still.'
'What do we do about her?'

‘We leave her alone… for now. If she becomes of any inconvenience, we will have to take her out.’
‘That is IF she ever becomes an inconvenience. We must refrain from doing evil as much as possible!’
‘Open your eyes man, this is an evil world we live in. People do not care about justice.’
‘But YOU DO, that is what matters. You need to be able to live with yourself, day after day.’
‘I admire your good heart man… just make sure nobody takes advantage of you!’
‘The same counts for you!’

2

The next morning, the vice-mayor of Matagalpa handed over the case to a detective who immediately inspected the library. This detective, 51-year-old *Juan Shaun y Valle*, inspected all the rooms and lastly, he founds the conference room where Fiona and Rensy had their love session. Juan served in the military for fifteen years and he was the father of two and grandfather of six. He was liberal minded, and he blamed the local tensions between the Matagalpa gangs and the locals on the conservative politics of the Bourbon Dynasty.
'Who rented this room yesterday?'
'Nobody, Sir. The log does not show any reservations.'
'According to eye-witnesses, Mister Sachéz came with a foreign woman.'
'Foreigner?'
'Yes, a tall one. Likely from Spain or France.', he checked around, 'It appears that Rensy Sanchéz broke in with the foreign lady.'
'Sir, do you mean that woman with that yellow dress?'
'How do you know that?'
'A week ago, there was a charity concert. The President of a Mayan-oriented foundation gave a speech, and she sang a song. She has been in town ever since. She walked around in yellow and white dresses.'
'Hmm…. Who is she?'
'Fiona Rodrigues y Olmeda, duchess of Amatique.'
'Thank you!'
The librarian left. Juan stayed in the conference room a bit longer to attempt to reconstruct what exactly happened in there and how that relates to the failed assassination.
A lot of stuff in the room was out of place. There were two glasses on the table, one bottle of rum that was half-full and the curtains on the window were half-open. The walked around to see if he could find any evidence. He was also confused by the amount of incense that was burned. It also surprised him that none of the librarians, nor the two Spanish troops, noticed the strong smell of incense coming from the room. He looked outside of the window and he realised that whoever stayed in that room had a perfect view on what was going on in the streets. While he was gazing from the window, another detective walked in.
'Sir?'

'Who are you?'
'*Justin Gonzales y Gonzales*, Sir. I have been appointed to assist you in this case.'
'Come in!'
The two detectives stood at the window, when Justin noticed that there was a handprint on the window.
'Sir… check this hand print here!'
'That appears like a female's hand.'
'Hands that were sweaty at the time of contact.'
'Hmmm…'
Juan turned around. He kneeled to inspect the sofa, where he suddenly encountered Fiona's panties, which she left behind, at the edge beneath the sofa.
'Mister Shaun…', he pointed towards the dried white drops on the carpet, 'that looks like semen to me… heading from the sofa towards the window.'
'Hmm… so the woman immediately left her lovers side shortly after he unloaded inside of her.'
'Maybe she was shocked by the gunfight outside.'
'I doubt it!'
Juan walked out of the conference room and he looked around on the second floor. Justin joined his side.
'Those two are not in town anymore…'
'How do you know that Sir?'
'I am experienced in this work, Mister Gonzales. Those two are on the run. Either we find them, or the wrong people do and they end up dead.'
That evening, the foundation crew arrived in Nicaragua's provincial capital where they entered their second office. The second office was seldom used by the foundation – it served as an additional archive of the foundation's activities and achievements. Mail coming from South America would arrive in their office in Leon, from where it would be picked up by assigned mail carriers, each three days, towards Guatemala City. The office had a dorm where the staff moved in. The staff hoped to stay there for at least a week before continuing to Guatemala City. Fiona moved into the office itself, together with Rensy. The next morning, several letters arrived – including a letter from Fiona's mother.
After reading the letter from her mother, Fiona realised that her life might take an unexpected turn she never asked for: Her father was

suspected of killing two politicians and for some weird reason she became a suspect too. She never visited Guadalajara; so, she had no idea how anyone could even think she had any involvement.
'Oh shit…'
'What is it?'
'I am the suspect of a double homicide.'
'What?!'
'It happened in Guadalajara past solstice. I was not there.'
'Then how are you a suspect?'
'My father is a suspect!'
'Oh my… did he do it?'
'I do not know.'
'I expected you to say, 'of course not!' or 'No way!''
'I know my father… he is not the best type of man you will meet.'
'Where is he?'
'He is in Guayaquil… my mum sent me the letter to inform me that the authorities might arrest me if they find any other reason to suspect me.'
'How could you be involved why you were not even in New Galicia at the time?'
'Well… that is what I need to find out!'
'The timing of this is weird.'
'What do you mean with that?'
'Right now, that you are prospering in your career, this accusation comes up. This is no coincidence.'
'Whatever it is… I am not going to worry about it. I have a foundation to look after and I got you now.'
'I get the feeling that this is far bigger than you realise.'
'I do not care about that, Rensy…'
'You should! You could get the death penalty if they convict you for murder!'
'That can never happen with the public knowledge that I was on another continent when the crime occurred.'
'If those creeps are brave enough to false accuse someone who was not even on the same continent, then they are able to come up with anything to incriminate you.'
'I will deal with it.'
'We will…'
'It does not concern you…'
'It does if we will stay together.'

'You are not the target', she embraced him, 'my father is... and I am probably used as some type of distraction to get his attention.'
'Tell me more about your father's business in New Galicia...'
'What can I tell you about it? He was a member of a knighthood over there... and he joined some meetings of them.'
'What I mean is', he released himself from her grip, 'was there any conflict he was involved with?'
'The last time I saw my father was over a year ago. I was in Panama City where he was awaiting the arrival of two French diplomats. He conflicted with some French importer who paid less for the goods than agreed.'
'You remember the names of the diplomats?'
'Well... Jules Vermont and Floris Gaulle. The diplomats arrived and he went into a conversation with them. From what I know, no solution was agreed. Dad still claimed that some French couple, from Toulouse, owed him 2.000 Spanish dollars.'
'That seems like an intense conflict.'
'Its sure is', she sat down, 'all the export of Quito is stored in Panama City, from where it is transported by land to a Caribbean port from where it continues to Europe.'
'Is that not ineffective?'
'There were plans for a canal in Panama ever since Charles I established the Spanish viceroyalties. We are 280 years further and there is still no canal in Panama.'
'Sometimes the Spanish are quite ineffective.'
'Tell me about it!'
'So... those two French diplomats tried to calm your father down.'
'It did not work... he was quite pissed.'
'Then... what if those two are involved in the crime.'
'That is a bit absurd.'
'I think not... if your father is a creditor and his debtors wanted to get rid of him... what better way is there to frame him in a crime?'
'All the way from France?'
'They imported from Spanish America, so they have a vested interest in keeping their doors open in the Spanish world. Having an exporter that badmouths them will not work in their favour.'
'Hmmm... you have a point!'
'I am not saying that is the case now...'

'It is something to consider. Just know, my father is a stubborn and embittered businessman. He often blames everything and everyone for his failures. Quite annoying!'
'You must be happy to be away from him!'
'I surely am…', she looked outside of the window, 'I plan to stay as long as possible in Guatemala.'
'I was born here… it is a beautiful country.'
'Hmm… have you ever left Guatemala?'
'Never.'
'You ever intend to move out?'
'Probably not… this country has everything anyone can wish for.'
'Like what?'
'Mountains, rivers, big, sweet lakes, wild animals, rainforest, white beaches… and urban centres.'
'Have you ever been to Guatemala City?'
'I have been to both the new and the old capital.'
'I really like Antigua Guatemala… such a shame that the Spanish government decided not to rebuild it!'
'It is the best that they did not rebuilt that place. It is in a dangerous place.'
'Which other places have you been to?'
'Leon, Grenada, El Realego, Juigalpa, Matagalpa, Cartago, San José, San Salvador, San Miguel, Santa Anta, San Cristobal, Huehuetenango, Trujillo, San Pedro Sula, Comayagua, Tegucigalpa and New Segovia….'
'You have been almost everywhere…'
'Yes… I love Guatemala and I am ready to fight and die for this kingdom.'
'I admire your patriotism.'
'What about you? You love Quito so much?'
'Hmm… my love is with Spain, which I see as my fatherland.'
'I cannot see Spain as my fatherland… I have never been there and I am not white…'
'Does that matter?'
'Well… it matters in society.'
'It does not matter to me.'
'You are the first one mentioning that it does not concern you. Peninsulares and criollos are praised above us natives and mestizos.'

‘For me… you are born under the Spanish flag, you are a Spaniard, just like me… quite simple.’
While they still spoke, one of the staff members came in with another package. It was from the royal governor. The package contained a ‘thank you’-letter and a donation of 100 Spanish dollars.
‘You are doing a good job with leading this foundation.’
‘Well… there are a lot of problems coming with it too.’
‘That is with everything in life.’
‘It probably is… I need to speak to Luis.’
‘Who is Luis?’
‘He is a farmer, from Oaxaca, that supports this foundation.’
‘Well… Oaxaca is at least one week riding away from here.’
‘I said I had to speak to him’, she crossed her legs, ‘not that I will speak with him instantly.’
‘What is there so urgent that you need to talk with him.’
‘I have the feeling he talked too much to the police.’
‘Hold on…’
‘My father is likely involved in some type of political violence. I do not rule that out.’
‘So… this Luis covers up for him?’
‘Kind off…’
‘If that is the case… it is likely Luis that also mentioned you.’
‘He may know more about Jules and Floris.’
‘Why is it that you cannot see that this case is a black hole that will suck you in?’
‘I am from a political family… so I know how bloody politics can become.’
‘Then… why do you not keep yourself out of it?’
‘I cannot keep myself out of it. My name was mentioned and now they are coming for me. So, I must be wise as a serpent to avoid getting caught.’
‘So, you are a fugitive then…’
‘To some extent, yes.’
‘I thought I was the one on the run.’
‘Not everything is what it seems, Rensy.’
He looked out of the window. He saw several men arguing in the streets.
‘Things are about to get ugly here...’, she came and looked out of the window too, ‘some people fighting.’

‘Such things often happen. Men often cannot handle their anger.’
‘Some women are out of line too!’
‘Well… but it is not women who run the world and I am glad we are not… it would be one emotional mess.’
‘Well… sodomite men are not any better.’
‘Tell that the all the empires since the Greeks that governed our species.’
‘Do not even talk about the ancient Greeks.’
‘All our leaders are Apollonian and Sodomites…’
‘I guess you are right. Nevertheless, I am glad I belong to the Spanish Empire…’
‘Me too!’
‘I am getting a bath!’
‘Where?’
‘There is a public bath nearby.’
‘No… that is a place where women wash their clothes publicly.’
‘Well… I will be washing myself there.’
‘Well… go for it!’
She laughed out loud. He left smiling.
Two hours later, detectives Juan and Justin arrived in Leon where they witnessed the police breaking up a brawl in the streets. Several men got hurt.
‘What is going on with this people…’
‘Guatemalans are often prone to violent crime… you should know that.’
‘I know…’
‘That is why the previous Captain General introduced so much entertainment to relieve the masses.’
‘Did it work?’
‘Well, the number of homicides per year decreased… but the amount of street violence increased…’
‘Criminals are quite competitive around here…’
‘Where do you think Fiona is hiding?’
‘She is not hiding anywhere’, he pointed to a building, ‘you see that building over there? There is where they are and that window there is the window of the Foundation’s second office.’
‘So, they have an office in Guatemala City as well as in Leon?’
‘Yes... the office in Leon is meant for the financial administration relating to the economic activities of the foundation in South America.’
‘What type of activities?’

'Collecting donations from exporters.'
'Why would the people from South America care about disadvantaged Mayans?
'They do not', she looked around, 'they care about the prestige of aiding disadvantaged Mayans… not about the Mayans themselves.'
'So… when will we go inside?'
'Right now!'
The two men parked their horses near the building and Juan knocked on the door. After a half minute, a tiny young man opened the door.
'Gentlemen?'
'Good evening… We are looking for Miss Rodrigues.'
'Come!'
The tiny man brought them to a room.
'Wait here…'
The tiny man entered in and he had a 1-minute conversation before leaving the room.
'You can enter in!'
'Thank you!'
The two detectives entered in, where they saw the tall and pale lady standing at the window, gazing into the streets.
'Sit down, officers!'
The gentlemen sat down. The desk had several books on them, a tiny Spanish flag, a book with Catholic prayer and a Mary statue.
'So… what can I do for you two?'
'We are here to investigate the homicide on two Matagalpa gang members. I am Juan Shaun y Valle, and this is my colleague Justin Gonzales y Gonzales.
'Nice to meet you two, detective Valle and detective Gonzales! About your visit: why are you wasting your time talking to me?', she turned around and walked towards the desk, where she sat down behind the desk, facing the two detectives, 'I am from a criollo family, located in Guayaquil, and I have been living here just for a small amount of time. I do not know any Matagalpans.'
'Well, actually… you do.'
'Then you know more about me than I do!'
'*Rensy Emanuel Sanchéz y Estevéz.* You met him at a café several days ago. You have been seen together at the library in Matagalpa.'
'That can be true, yes.'

‘So, you acknowledge being with him in one of the conference rooms of the library?’
‘Yes, Sir.’
‘What were you doing there?’
‘Nothing special’, she made eye contact with Juan, ‘I was just a horny woman who found a handsome man to satisfy my deep thirst for physical intimacy.’
‘Did he satisfy you?’
‘He sure did!’
‘You are incredibly open about it.’
‘There is nothing to be ashamed off. That is how I am built.’
‘Well, your lover…’
‘Just call him Rensy, please.’
‘Well… Rensy is related to three Matagalpan chiefs and he is also the target of contention by one of the Matagalpan gangs.’
‘Again… what does that has to do with me?’
‘That afternoon, in that library… could have become your last! There was a hit on Rensy’s life after being seen with you. So, the man you are with now carries danger with him.’
‘I thought so…’
‘You are the head of a charity foundation if I am correct?’
‘Indeed, the Santa Barbara Foundation for The Felicity of Mayans of the Kingdom of Guatemala.’
‘That is a fancy name.’
‘We are Spanish… we love long fancy, Catholic names!’
‘What we also love is law and order.’
‘Detectives… if there is anything you need to know about what happened to those gang members, then you have to speak to Rensy yourself.’
‘Where is he?’
‘He went to the public pond to wash himself.’
‘In the public pond?!’
‘Well… that is what he said.’
‘He is out of his mind!’
‘I told him it was not a good idea… but he is a bit stubborn, I guess.’
‘Did he ever tell you about his past and his family?’
‘Not much… we have not known each other for that long.’
‘But you have known him long enough to sleep with him?’

'I have my reasons why I opened my thighs for him… I am sure he is a good man on the inside. Exactly what I need.'
'Be sure that he is really Godsent and not a distraction.'
'If you want to find him, you need to go to the public pond.'
'We will… thank you for your time!'
'¡De nada!'
The two left the building.
'Are they gone?'
'Yes', she began writing a letter, 'you can come out of that wardrobe.'
'Finally!'
'Tell me the truth…'
'I told you…'
'Tell me', she looked at him sternly, 'did you have anything to do with the killing of those men?'
'No…'
'Is there anything else you need to say, you better do it now before I have to find out myself.'
'I have nothing to report, ma'am.'
'Look, I have to be strict on who I bring with me in this foundation. There is a lot that depends on this foundation.'
'I get it…'
'I want you to also do some work for the foundation. It would be odd if people see you around me all the time, without you contributing to anything.'
'What can you do?'
'You can do some of my tasks, while I… the lady… take a step back.'
'But…'
'Women are not made for roles like this… it is quite exhausting. A man is a far more capable of managing this than I do.'
'Then…I will do my best.'
'You will manage it informally, while formally I remain president… but I just want a man to cuddle man and empower me. I do not want to be the head.'
'I get it.'
'So… what do you think we should do next, Mr. President?'
'We need to continue to Guatemala City right away!'
'Yes, Sir!'

3

Amadeo II was released from custody and he returned to his estate in Guayaquil. At arrival, his managers informed him of an infection that plagued some of the slaves.
'How long has this infection been around?'
'Just several weeks, Sir.'
'Any idea where it came from?'
'There were some East Indian slaves that were imported by some cartels from Peru… and one of those East Indian slaves had a weird cold… and that is where it came from.'
'I do not understand why they long for slaves from the East Indies… we already have enough slaves around and we get enough from Africa, for God's sake!'
'Well, East Indian slaves are far cheaper and less likely to revolt.'
'But they are not as good on the field…'
'Well… some Spanish people long for East Indians on their fields.'
'That is why we have an infectious disease now in our cities. My goodness…'
'Sir, there is another thing.'
'What?'
'Your daughter is also a suspect.'
'How can that be? She has nothing to do with this!'
'Well, not according to the detectives in Guatemala.'
'Fiona is INNOCENT!'
'Convince the authorities in Guatemala about that.'
'Has she been arrested?'
'She messaged your wife that she has been interviewed by two detectives.'
'What are their names?'
'Juan Shaun y Valle and Justin Gonzales y Gonzales. The interview happened six days ago in Leon, Province of Nicaragua. She wrote the letter just minutes after the men left and the letter was shipped the same day to Guayaquil.'
'No wonder it arrived so quickly!'
'What will you do now, Sir?'
'It appears I will have to visit Guatemala gain.'
'Alone?'
'No… I will bring some backup with me!'

'Sir… there is something else.'
'What?'
'You got a warning from Mister Muriyama.'
'What does he want?'
'Your latest shipment to a Shanghai-based family was seized by the Chinese government and the family has been placed in detention for two months. It was after the swift intervention by Taro that the family was released, and their cargo returned to them. Shipments to China must go via the Spanish protocols that the Chinese ágreed with the Council of the Indies.'
'Man… that Taro is one annoying figure.'
'He wants to prevent trouble in Spanish exports to Asia.'
'I know… I know', he read Taro's letter, 'I will message him later. First, I need to gather my team before we sail to El Realejo!'
Meanwhile, detectives Juan and Justine found out that Fiona received 2.000 Spanish Real[1] hush money from two French diplomats that were appointed to Mexico City. The money was intended for her to withhold information about her father's business from her father. She agreed to keep the news that her father was defrauded a secret in exchange for the hush money. The two detectives received permission from their superiors to travel to Mexico City to interrogate the two diplomats. The two men arrived in the Spanish vice-regal capital, form where North America has been governed for almost three centuries by the Spanish Crown.
The two detectives were declined by the French Embassy, which meant that they were not able to interview the two French diplomats. This was in line with international law, as agreed between the Crowns in Europe, that diplomats were immune from the laws where they were deployed to. While being in Mexico City, the two detectives requested the Spanish State to remove the French Embassy from the Viceroyalty of New Spain. However, that same hour the secretary of the Viceroy informed them that the removal of the French Embassy could only happen on behalf of the king or if the Viceroy considered the French diplomats to pose a threat to public safety. The two detectives were frustrated that their investigation was being frustrated by the government.
That same evening, right before the men planned to return to the Captaincy General of Guatemala, they received assistance from a

[1] In today's money €12.750

Portuguese diplomat who was aware about the scandal surrounding the death of the two Spanish politicians as well as the fraud that befell Amadeo II.
'Sir, why did you decide to come to us?'
'Amadeo II is not a friend of Portugal nor the Portuguese people… in 1796 he agreed to coverup the seizing of two Portuguese ships near Guayaquil. The two ships assisted British cargo from the Kingdom of Quito towards British India… the seizing of the ships led to the death of 120 Portuguese nationals… the seizing was illegal and not sanctioned by the Spanish viceroys. Amadeo was involved in the seizing and he did whatever he could to cover it up.'
'Oh God…'
'So, Portuguese envoys are all informed about that man.'
'Got it!'
'So… I have something on this man that you might not be aware off…'
'What is it?'
'Amadeo II's mother is *Fiona Felipa Camões da Costa*. She is the daughter of a Portuguese treasurer that managed several projects during the reforms of former Prime Minister Sebastião José de Carvalho e Melo… during the rule of Joseph I. However, after slavery was abolished in continental Portugal, some of the Portuguese slaveowners requested help from Spanish slave owners to rent 'migrant workers' to Portugal. Amadeo II's father was involved in this scam.'
'So, they were renting out their slaves to Portuguese farms…and the wage of those workers went to the Spanish slave owners?'
'Indeed!'
'So… what happened?'
'The scam was figured out after a slave died of exhaustion… Fiona's father, *Raul Camões*, was arrested. His daughter forced herself on Amadeo II's father and Amadeo was born out of this union. The couple married quickly when she was proven to be pregnant…'
'Why did she do that?'
'She managed to blackmail her new family-in-law to pay for the legal fees of her father… the bribes worked. Amadeo II's father has been banned from ever entering Portuguese territory: he will be arrested, and he can face execution if he is ever prosecuted.'
'Prosecution for extortion?'
'Prosecution for murder and human trafficking.'

'What relevancy has that with the issue of the two Spanish victims in Guadalajara?'
'The two killed politicians were investigating the financial activities of Amadeo II and his family in New Spain as well as New Granada... and I do not know that much about what they found out... but they found out enough to shut down the Dukedom of Amatique for good.'
'Ah... now we are getting somewhere!'
'The two men just handed in their receipt at the court of Guadalajara who would further investigate the matter... it was just days after the men handed in their receipts that they disappeared.'
'What happened to the receipts?'
'They are still at the court.'
'Hmm.... That is weird.'
'Look... I do not know exactly what they found out... but it was a scandal big enough that it might cause the whole dukedom of the Rodrigues Household to be abolished.'
'What can cause the Crown to make such a decision?'
'Either... it is genocide or treason to the king. At least, that is what I can think of.'
'Treason...'
'Well, it is up to you two what you do with it.'
'Thank you, Sir. We will take it from here.'
When the Portuguese diplomat left, the two men decided not to return to Guatemala, but to continue to the court of Guadalajara to figure out more about the case.
Meanwhile, across the Atlantic Ocean several investors in the Santa Barbara Foundation held a meeting to discuss the future of their undertaking. The foundation was funded by two Spanish families –the *Ramos* and the *Dominguez* – from Galicia, with the assistance of the Royal Audiencia of Guatemala. The two families used the foundation to launder their income from the British settlements in the Caribbean. This was their clever way of exploiting British merchandise as well as avoiding the number of tariffs they had to pay to the Spanish customs.
Theo Ramos, who arranged the legal affairs of the Ramos Household, considered it odd how the revenue of the foundation decreased over time. He was convinced that either their coverup was discovered or that someone was sabotaging their efforts.
'Gentlemen, since the time we created the *Santa Barbara Foundation for the Alleviation of The Mayans of The Kingdom of Guatemala*, which

was proposed by my great-uncle *Juan Ramos y Xair*, who has a Mayan mother, we have been able to retain our income from the British possessions in the Caribbean without having to pay any of the customs we owe the Spanish Crown. The foundation itself has sufficient donors and it does bring relief to Mayan towns throughout Guatemala. So, therefore we were never discovered. However, since past two years… we see a decrease in revenue of at least 63%. This is bothersome.'
'Maybe some of the donors donated less…'
'The foundation also provides commercial activities that bring more revenue than donors donate… it is those reports that we always use to launder our income… with the decrease of revenue… we will lose the loophole we depend on.'
'What did the latest report say?'
'The President told us that she would attempt to gain support, for the foundation, in the Province of Nicaragua.'
'Hmm… who is the current President anyway?'
'It is a woman, Fiona Rodrigues…'
'Since when do we entrust our financial affairs to a woman?'
'She is the daughter of Gregorio Rodrigues, who is a duke in the Viceroyalty of New Granada.'
'Even if she is from a noble background, we should not entrust our affairs to a woman… that is too risky.'
'The donors as well as the Royal Audiencia in Guatemala City agreed to this.'
'Hold on…', someone from the Dominguez Household interfered, 'Is this Gregorio Rodrigues not the same man who is suspected of putting a hit on the two Spanish politicians that were killed in Guadalajara?'
'He is a suspect indeed… but none of the Spanish courts in Spanish America have been able to convict him.'
'We should have been consulted about this… now we have the daughter of a potential traitor and criminal guiding the foundation… that will be reason enough for the government to put us under investigation.'
'That will take some time…'
'That means we need to deal with this right away.'
'Remain calm everyone!'
'We do not know who this Fiona Rodrigues is…'
'She has no bad reputation.'
'Her father does and sooner or later that will rub off on her too… and on us.'

‘What we can do is to make her an offer…’
‘What offer can we make her? She already had access to all our affairs.’
‘Then we must be patient, should we not?’
‘Hold on’, one of the Dominguez Household members came in with news, ‘we just got news from Guatemala.’
‘What is it?’
‘Fiona signed a contract with a French importer of indigenous fruits. De *Dessalines* Household from Port-au-Prince. The agreement is disastrous… now local Mayan chiefs will make more money, on our backs, then we will get revenue from our import from British possessions.’
‘It is a charity foundation… not a Mayan Financial Ministry!’
‘The Dessalines are not the most trustworthy of French families.’
‘Which French family are you aware off that is reliable when it comes to international trade?’
‘We need to get a better grip on that foundation.’
‘Who is the current treasurer?’
‘An Italian guy named *Balduno Danilo Casighari*. He is from Sardinia.’
‘Hmm…. The Casigharis are not a threat to us. They are pro-Spain, and they offer much supply for many Spanish sailors.’
‘So… we have an asset in there. That will work out well.’
‘6.000 Spanish Real[2] was missing from the treasury of the foundation. Balduno concluded that the money vanished within a period of two weeks… before this report was sent to us.’
‘6.000 Spanish Real… that is a lot.’
‘Hmm… what do we do now?’
‘Offer her another job.’
‘What type of job?’
‘A job in Spain.’
‘No no no… she is not likely to leave Spanish America for this contentious Iberian Peninsula. I would not either.’
‘Maybe we can start another foundation in Santo Domingo and ask her to become the President of it.’
‘What are we going to call it? There are no charity needs on Santo Domingo. Have you forgotten that His Majesty conceded the Captaincy General of Santo Domingo to France in 1795?’
‘There is still a huge Spanish speaking population there…’

[2] In today’s money €38.250

‘So, you want a charity organisation in a French colony? Do not forget that there is a huge revolt going on in Saint Dominigue now…’
‘Soon, the French will find a way to deal with that.’
‘Do you seriously think that the new French consul, Bonaparte, will be able to deal with those revolting negroes in Saint Dominigue?’
‘He will have to… or else… both France and Spain will lose face… worldwide!’
‘So, when are we going to the authorities to establish our new foundation?’
‘We will have to go to the French Embassy in Madrid to establish this.’
‘Hmmm… that might take long now that France is in a mess.’
‘Maybe we can just use our current foundation and extend its activities into Saint-Dominigue?’
‘That is a better option!’
‘Good!’
‘What do we do about those 6.000 coins that went missing?’
‘That Casighari boy can deal with it… he can even report Fiona Rodrigues if he suspects that she is stealing from the foundation.’
‘Spain’s duchess is about to fall very soon…’
‘You mean… Quito’s duchess… she was born in Quito.’
‘She is still from Spanish America…’
‘But not from our beloved peninsula…’
‘Enough! Roberto, Juan, Julio, Giovanni and Raphael… offer the duchess a new position in Saint-Dominigue and meanwhile we will figure something out for our cover.’
‘Yes, Sir!’
The same hour, Juan posted a job offer to the address of the Santa Barbara Foundation. The captain told him that the letter would likely arrive in just four or four and a half weeks’ time due to the fast wind on the Atlantic Ocean that season.
A day later, the Dominguez Household received a threat from the Rodrigues Household, of which Fiona was a part. The Rodrigues Household, which was seated in Seville, Cartagena de Indias and Guayaquil, loaned 45.000 Spanish Real[3] to the Dominguez Household to bail each other out from several failed shipments. Seventeen shipments of both households were seized by British privateers between 1781 and 1787. The agreement was that with monthly instalments the Dominguez Household would pay back the Rodrigues Household. Until

[3] In today’s money €286.875

now, only 20.000 was paid from February 1790 till February 1799. The Dominguez Household covered up their 'delay' of payments with various excuses. The head of the Sevillian part of the Rodrigues Household decided to put a hit on some of the men of the Dominguez Household if before the end of 1800 the loan was not fully repaid.
The reason for this pressure was to coverup the violent division within the Rodrigues Family: those from Cartagena de Indias and Guayaquil opposed the Iberian-centred politics of those that resided in Seville. The Sevillian branch of the Rodrigues Household invested much money in Spanish warfare as well as migration projects to the Nootka Territory. The Guayaquilean and Cartagenero branches of the Rodrigues Household longed to invest the family's wealth into better infrastructure in South America to boost the economy in the Viceroyalty of New Granada – where many remote towns had no direct access to the Spanish highways. The Guayaquilean and Cartagenero branches wanted all the towns in New Granada to be better connected to the ports so that all the inhabitants of the colony were able to participate in the economy. The Sevillian branch considered the military defence of the empire to be of higher importance than 'welfare' to the least 'advanced' people.
By showing 'leadership' in coercing payments from the Dominguez Household the head of the Sevillian branch, *Lionel Mattias Rodrigues y Camões*, hoped to unite the family again.
Lionel also informed the other heads, *Gregorio* (Amadeo II) and *Lucas*, about his decision. Both Gregorio and Luca agreed with Lionel's decision. Lionel's wife, Mathilde, requested permission to visit Fiona in Guatemala. Even though Lionel was not fond of the idea, he still permitted her to go – assisted by eight mercenaries as her protection.
What Lionel was not aware off was that his wife wanted to visit her former lover, Calvin de Aragon, whom she met in Oaxaca in 1783. She was not aware that Calvin already passed away for a while.
While Lionel's wife prepared for her journey across the Atlantic, the authorities in Guadalajara requested Fiona's arrest. The judge, however, dismissed the petition because she was not residing within the jurisdiction of the Kingdom of New Galicia. When the authorities challenged the judges' decision in the Royal Audiencia of Guadalajara, the authorities of the intendancy were vindicated: Fiona had to be arrested, but only after consent from the Royal Audiencia of Guatemala, which functioned without any factual supervision from the Viceroyalty of New Spain. Meanwhile, Fiona and her team attended a wedding in

San Vicente. One of the donors died three weeks prior to his son's wedding. The son, *Felipe Juan Joachim de Jaén y Maria* (1782-1824) married a woman named *Tamara Martina Rodriguez y Espiño* (1778-1824), who was the grand niece of Fiona's uncle *Victor Vicente Rodriguez y Toledo* (1753-1829) who lived next to Amadeo II's estate.
Felipe, after meeting Fiona at his wedding, sensed that bad news was coming for her.
'Miss Rodrigues, maybe you should leave Guatemala for a while…'
'Leaving Guatemala?'
'I sense that some danger is brewing against you now.'
'You are a psychic?'
'Kind off… and I am seldom wrong about what my intuition picks up.'
'What type of danger do you sense against me.'
'I feel like someone close to you is about to betray you anytime soon.'
'Hmm… that might be true. My father has some enemies that seek to bring him down.'
'I am not sure if its your father…'
'In any case, I will consider your warning.'
Just several minutes later, she vomited twice, and she decided to visit a physician the next day. The physician confirmed that Fiona was two months' pregnant of Rensy's child.
'Two months already?!'
'Yeah… you met him exactly 8 weeks ago, right?'
'Yes… it was when we had sex for the first time.'
'You were on the high of your fertility cycle… so congratulations!'
'Eh… thanks! I just need to find a way to tell him.'
'Where is he?'
'He is in town, with me… we attended a wedding of a distant relative of mine.'
'Inform him. I am sure he will be happy to hear about it!'
'I will.'
That evening, Fiona informed him about her pregnancy after they had intercourse together.
'What?!'
'You heard me… we are becoming parents.'
'I… I… never expected it to happen.'
'I hope it is a girl… she will be just as pretty as me.'
'What will you call her?'
'I am not sure… maybe Olivia… or Carmen. I will thank about it.'

‘What will your father say now you are having this child without a wedding ring on your finger?’
‘I will deal with him later… what is important now is that I focus on the well-being of this baby.’
‘Will you move back to Guayaquil to give birth?’
‘I will give birth right over here… in Guatemala. No need to go back to give birth to it. By the way, it is your child too… so, I do not want to withhold the baby from you.’
‘Thanks.’
‘Besides… there is visit coming tomorrow.’
‘Visit?’
‘There is a Vietnamese merchant coming to Guatemala with his family. The kingdom of Viet has agreed to trade with Spanish America back in the 1780s… so every year a fleet with Vietnamese merchants arrive in Acajutla, Acapulco and Guayaquil.’
‘What do you know about this merchant?’
‘His name is Mihn… and he comes with his wife, five daughters and four servants.’
‘What is he trading?’
‘Textile...’
‘Then Guatemala is the right place for him.’
‘They are estimated to arrive in Acajutla around 18:00 tomorrow… so we need to be there to welcome them.’
‘How accurate is that estimation?’
‘The ship departed from Acapulco two days ago… on 19:45...’
‘Hmm… then tomorrow is the right time.’
‘Will you come with me?’
‘Sure!’

4

It was around 14:20 when the harbour master informed Fiona that a ship was approaching. The couple went to the pier where the Galleon ship arrived at the pier. The two of them saw various Southeast Asian people come off the ship and eventually, he saw a small man, next to a small woman, approaching her.
'Ma'am, are you Miss Rodrigues?'
'Yes...', she was happy, 'welcome to Guatemala!'
'It is an honour to be here! This is my wife, Nam Chi.'
'Nice to meet you, Nam Chi!'
'Our daughters are still coming off the ship… where can we lodge?'
'We will travel to the capital by tonight. Meanwhile, you can stay at the guesthouse over there.'
'Good!'
The Vietnamese couple moved to the guesthouse where they received a room for the remainder of the day. Shortly afterwards, their daughters came off the ship: *Hoa, Hang, Chau, Cam* and *Huyên*. The oldest was Huyên: she was a 27-years-old maker of bronzeware. This was her second time in Spanish America: the first time was 1794 when she visited the Viceroyalty of Peru, the Kingdom of Chile, and the Viceroyalty of New Granada with her uncle, who became an officer in the Spanish Navy. It was a journey of five months that began with their arrival in Guayaquil. She visited al the mayor cities of the three Spanish possessions. The second time she visited Spanish America was in 1798, when she spent two months in the Nootka Territory as part of an envoy of another uncle of hers (who sought trade with Spanish exporters). That time, she eventually visited Mexico City and Guatemala City, before departing back to Asia via the port of Acajutla. In total she spent three and a half months in the Viceroyalty of New Spain. Her two uncles were al seniors and the only ones of her family that managed to escape the poor rural life of their background. Her father managed to become a merchant with the aid of his two elder brothers who also thought him Spanish.
Huyên was glad that her father would stay in Spanish America for a half year to trade – and that he would bring his whole family with him. All Huyên siblings were from her father's second marriage. There was an age difference of eight years between her father's second child, Hoa. The youngest of them was fourteen years old, Hang. Huyên got along

well with her younger siblings, but she remained reclusive towards them.
That night, the Vietnamese household, as well as the couple, travelled in chariots to the capital. The evening after arriving in Guatemala City, Fiona received a letter from her father in which he requested her to not talk to any of the authorities concerning the case of the murdered Spanish politicians. She put the letter aside as soon as possible. She did not want to be bothered with the political dramas of her father.
While sitting behind her desk, someone knocks on the door.
'Come in…'
A tall, copper skinned, woman entered in. She wore a white dress that revealed her feminine figure.
'Can I help you, Ma'am?'
She handed over a piece of paper to Fiona. There was written in both Spanish and Chinese:

Ma'am, my name is Huyên Nyu, my father is the merchant that came for trade. I do not speak Spanish very well... would you like to keep me company? I would like to have a new friend.

Fiona laughed and she nodded to the woman. Huyên understood the confirmation of Fiona.
'Sit next to me… and help me with these envelops, please.'
Huyên set next to her, on another chair, and she understood quickly what Fiona wanted from her. The two did not speak at all. While the two worked on the documents, a priest knocked on the door.
'Father Roger!'
'Fiona… who is she?'
'This is Huyên… she is my new receptionist. I am just working her in.'
'Well, you might need a receptionist…'
'Why?'
'They are looking for you… the authorities.'
'What?'
'There is an arrest warrant against you.'
'WHAT?!'
'Fear not… it might take a while before the Royal Audiencia of this capital decides on the matter. Just know that you are listed as a suspect.'
'Oh my…'
'Just remain low key coming weeks… and avoid trouble.'
'I will, father.'

The priest left.
'It is quite embarrassing. My dad is involved with some crooked businessman. Now, they suspect me of involvement in the killing of those two politicians. I have nothing to do with it. Anyway, we are done here… let us get something to drink.'
The two left Fiona's office and they arrived at an indigenous bar nearby. Fiona ordered two Mayan beverages. While the two drank their beverages, Rensy arrived on a mule.
'What are you doing here with the Vietnamese's daughter?'
'She needs a friend around her, and she does not speak Spanish.'
'Maybe it is time for her to learn Spanish… that is quite important for her coming half year.'
'She will be around us...'
'Is that a good idea?'
'Why do you ask?'
'She seems a bit… needy.'
'For what?'
'Attention… look how she is dressed.'
'There is warm weather here…'
'Similar to her homeland.'
'You are interested in her?'
'Eh… no. I am not.'
'Then do not worry how she is dressed.'
'Got it!'
At the same time, a Chinese trader appeared at the bar. His name was *Weng Jung*, a 34-year-old father of three daughters: *Lanfeng* (2), *Raifeng* (4) and *Liu* (7). His wife, *Ting*, stayed at home with the children while he crossed the seas to earn his income. This is his first time in Spanish America. He spoke Spanish due to living in The Philippines for over a decade.
'A little bottle of beer, please!'
'Hold on!'
The bartender gave him the bottle of beer. His eyes fell on Huyên. He then saw that Fiona came back and sat next to her. Jung made up from the way interacted that the copper skinned woman was either the slave or servant of the brunette lady. He followed them to the Foundation's building where Fiona offered a room to Huyên as accommodation. The following week, Jung followed Huyên's every move. He even broke into the Foundation's building to spy on her during the evenings. He

was so swift in his movements that nobody noticed him being in the building.
Eight days after Huyên arrived at the Foundation, she went into the garden to get a shower under the artificial waterfall. The garden of the Foundation was seldom visited by anyone. While she was showering, Jung disguised himself as house cleaner and he gazed at her from a corner. When she finished showering, she noticed footprints that were not hers. However, she did not freak out about it. She dried herself and she walked to her room instead.
Later that day, she informed one of the staff members in broken Spanish that she thinks someone broke in. The staff member appointed the new employee, Jerry, to patrol the hall at night. This jerry was nobody else but Jung who requested a job at the Foundation under a false identity. Jung also spoke the Viet language and he got acquainted with his target swiftly. Just three days later, Fiona noticed that Huyên was close with the new employee. She thought it was cute. That day she came back from a meeting in Quetzaltenango where she arranged a meeting between the Vietnamese couple and several Mayan textile producers.
This day, Fiona felt lazy, and she decided to ask Huyên to perform an exotic dance for her, while a Black female servant would play the flute. Huyên was glad to perform. The Black female servant considered Fiona's request to be quite weird and inappropriate. However, as the servant girl… she just got along and played the flute.
While Binc moved her hips sensually, Fiona drank some strong cider that she purchased on the market in Quetzaltenango just two days earlier.
'Move those hips… sweety! Move them!', she shouted while becoming tipsy, 'There you go…'
After Fiona finished her last cup of cider, the Black servant saw a familiar spirit entering Fiona's pelvis and she suddenly saw Fiona undressing herself. The Black servant felt the urge to get out of the situation as soon as possible. However, she was still not done with the song. Fiona eventually joined the dance, naked, while Huyên also wore the thin dress she always wore. Fiona did not actually dance at all. She just moved around Binc a little bit before passing out on the couch. After the song was done, the Black servant left the room as soon as possible. Jung heard the music stop and he decided to check out what happened. When he approached the stairs, he encountered this Black woman running away.

'Ma'am… why are you running away?'
'Do not get involved… leave the President alone!'
'What?'
'Leave her alone… she is not in her right mind now!'
The black woman left the building.
Jung moved to Fiona's office slowly and there she found Fiona sleepin on the couch, naked, while Huyên stared outside of the window. Fiona fell asleep due to being drunk. Huyên did not even notice how odd the situation was. Jung knocked on the door.
[he spoke Vietnamese to Huyên]
'Ma'am… is the President all right?'
'She is just a bit drunk… she asked me to dance for her… so I did.'
'Hmm… when do you think she will wake up?'
'I have no idea…'
'Come… let her rest of a while.'
'You are right… hold on.'
Huyên left the room and she invited Jung over to her room. The room was tiny with a small window covered by a yellow curtain. There Huyên became carnal with Jung, not knowing who he really was.
Fiona woke up an hour later and she did not even remember what happened before she passed out. She later checked the bottle to find out that it was alcoholic free cider. She was surprised that her mind tricked her into drunkenness even though she did not even drink a drop of alcohol. She noticed she was naked, and she dressed herself quickly.
By now, the familiar spirit left her body and wandered back to her parent's house in Guayaquil: the entity has been following her since birth. The open access that enabled the evil spirit [to remain attached to Fiona] was Fiona's excessive neediness for attention that was becoming pathological. Due to her good looks, sweet voice and her noble background people excused the neediness as something eccentric. She was not even aware that her own behaviour was becoming self-destructive. However, she had no real friends around her to alert her about the path she was on.
When she was dressed, she walked to Huyên room where she saw her and the new employee, beneath the blankets. She closed the door quietly and she went outside for some fresh air.
When she was outside, she saw Brittany and Josephine. Brittany and Josephine were two British peers that moved to Guatemala in 1795 to participate in the Spanish trade with Japan. The two women know each

other since their mid-teens, and they consider each other family. Josephine comes from a butcher's family, in Oxford, and she met Brittany during a festival near London. Brittany came from a carpenter's household and she craves knowledge as well as financial autonomy (something that was considered weird for a woman at the time). The two friends decided to board to Spanish America to start a new life as adventurers. Past years, the women became acquainted with the Foundation and in 1798 the two became friends with Fiona.
'Ah… is that not Fiona?'
'It is me, al right…'
'Who is that Asian girl that has been around you lately?'
'You mean Huyên? She is the daughter of a Vietnamese merchant that arrived in Guatemala for trade.'
'Hmm…. She is very well shaped.'
'Come on, Josephine… what are you looking at?'
'Well, I always check out such stuff… just like I always check out you.'
'Well, thanks again. Just know that she is involved with a new employee.'
'Which one?'
'A guy called Jerry Kinston. He is British too... well, at least… born in a British territory.'
'Which ethnicity is he?'
'Chinese I believe.'
'Sad, I would like to get acquainted with her.'
'Feel free to do so, ladies… just do not startle her. She does not speak Spanish that well nor English.'
'Who does speak English in this world?'
'In any case… what are you doing around here?'
'There was a body found…'
'A body?'
'Near the French shop… the body of a Mayan woman… twenty-three years old… mother of three…'
'Oh gosh!'
'The Royal Audiencia thinks it was a political assignation.'
'Political assassination?'
'Some of the Mayan chieftains just pleaded for more provincial autonomy in Spain… so if that is granted, some of the plantation owners will lose power over society… so, the Royal Audiencia thinks that this Mayan lady became the target of a political rivalry.'

‘What is the evidence?’
‘I am not sure… but that is what they are aiming at.’
‘This is not something beneficial for the peace around here.’
‘Well, Guatemalans have been prone to violent crime anyway… that is why Charles III came with the Bourbon Reforms to grant local autonomy and more economic opportunities to the locals.’
‘It did work… but still…’
‘Some things are not meant to be solved, Fiona. Let it go.’
‘In any case… keep me informed about the matter, please.’
‘We will dear…’
Fiona walked away. Josephine stared at her while she walked away. Josephine was a bit short, while Brittany was quite tall. Both looked and even sounded similar.
‘Why do you keep staring at her?’
‘She has a good figure, Brit…’
‘Sure… but… she has a guy, remember?’
‘Ah well… she might change her mind.’
‘Do not even go there… she is carrying his baby.’
‘How do you know?’
‘You did not know? She told it a week ago… I believe.’
‘If it is a daughter… she will be just a sweet as her mum.’
‘If it is a daughter, I hope she will have a better attitude then her mum.’
‘Fiona is not a bad woman…’
‘She is however… to naïve…’
‘Ok… I know… but…’
‘No buts… Josephine… especially if you are a parent. I often asked myself what she saw in that Rensy guy. He is from a thuggish background. She should not even be involved with him.’
‘Maybe she wants to break away from her relatives…’
‘While going around calling herself duchess…’
‘She might not want to be tied to someone her father has in mind.’
‘I think that might have been better for her.’
‘Yeah… but… at the other hand, she knows what type of family she has.’
‘By the way… what do we actually know about the Mayan woman that was killed?’
‘She had several stab wounds… so people think it was a personal conflict that escalated.’
‘Hmmm… personal conflict.’

‘I think it has to do with that Public Affairs Officer of the Santa Barbara Foundation.’
‘What about him?’
‘Carlo… has been sleeping around with her.’
‘What? Since when?’
‘For about two years now.’
‘Two whole years… for Christ’s sake…’
‘Well, that is not all… Carlo received a large sum of money from some French Revolutionary soldier a month ago.’
‘A revolutionary soldier?’
‘The soldier turned against Louis XVI and he joined the newly founded Republic of France in 1790… the soldier, however, fled France two years ago after the French judge convicted him to ten years of hard labour for smuggling white slave girls from Russia.’
‘Oh gosh…’
‘The soldier sailed to Veracruz and from there he moved slowly to Guatemala City… he is now secretly tricking indigenous women into prostitution. Indigenous women, from Spanish America, are desired in brothels in Europe…’
‘Oh dear… does Fiona know about this?’
‘Probably not…’
‘She is the President of a foundation that seeks to alleviate impoverished Mayan communities and she has a human trafficker that kidnaps Mayan girls on her team? She needs to know about it!’
‘If she does not know about it, it might be better if she remains ignorant about it… she is pregnant, a bit mentally ill and she is trapped by wolves in sheep’s clothing!’
‘True…’
‘What is important now is that Carlo is exposed for the hypocrite and creep he really is.’
‘What is the name of that French captain?’
‘I believe… his last name is Toulon… or something like that.’
‘Jacques-Marie Toulon?’
‘Yeah…’
‘Hmm… I think he is a supporter of an Italian guy called Napoleon… who took over the French republic recently.’
‘Whoever he is supporting or loathing… that is not our concern. Our concern is that he is taking advantage of the kindness of others to make money.’

'Mister Toulon is not even the real problem. Carlo is… Carlo should know better.'
'What do we do about this?'
After a little silence, Brittany grabbed Josephine and dragged her with her to Carlo's office.
'What are we doing around here?'
'Shhhh… trust me.'
The door opened. A tall Italian man opened the door, with sleepy eyes, and a smell of alcohol.
'What is going on, Brittany?'
'We need you to do us a favour?'
'What type of favour?'
'Josephine has a cousin, in Britain, who really wants to have some Mayan jewellery… can you arrange a good deal for us?'
'Why do you not ask Fiona?'
'She is occupied now. She has relationship issues with her man.'
'The two are not even legally married and they already have issues… and she is pregnant… anyway… I can see what I can do for you.'
'Do you know any French merchant that can transport it for us to Britain? If a French ship does it, the taxes will be different… due to the alliance between France and Spain.'
'Hmmm…. correct. Look, I know this guy… his name is Toulon. He is a terribly busy man. He is about to sail to Europe within several days. I will contact him as soon as possible to figure out if he can carry some cargo for you to Britain.'
'Oh… that would be great.'
'In this case, I will pay the jewellery from the treasury of the foundation and later… Josephine can pay the foundation back.'
'That will be good.'
'This is not something we usually do, and we are not even allowed to do it… so keep this quiet! Ok?'
'Great!'
'Then there is another thing…'
'What?'
'Beware of that man Fiona is sleeping with.'
'Rensy?'
'Yeah… Who else?'
'Why?'

'Look... I am not a saint. I admit that... but this man... he is bad news. Believe me... stay away from him!'
'We had no intention of being involved with him anyway.'
'Are you sure you are not horny for him?'
'We are horny... but not for him.'
'Well, that is fine then. Is there anything else, ladies?'
'When will we hear from you?'
'Come back the day after tomorrow... in the afternoon. If you can, bring 10 Spanish Real with you... just tribute for the captain.'
'Sure!'
'Please, get out of this place before people begin to ask why you were here.'
'Sure...'
The two ladies left the foundation's building.
When the ladies arrived outside, the saw Fiona walking towards them.
'Fiona...'
'Hey girls... can you keep me company tonight? I just want to go to the theatre or to some concert.'
'Sure...'
'I will pay.'
'You mean, the foundation will pay.'
'Do not worry about it.'

5

While Brittany, Josephine and Fiona enjoyed the theatre play, Jacques-Marie and Carlo met near the townhall of the capital. Jacques-Marie brought some custom's papers that Carlo had to sign.
'It is good you have the papers.'
'I am a bit behind schedule… I should have departed to Bermuda Isle last week.'
'The wind is in your favour anyway…'
'Yeah… but I want to get to Britain first and from next week there is another Spanish fleet that patrols the waters between Florida and Cuba… so, that is why I wanted to depart last week.'
'You cannot do that anymore anyway… so when will you depart.'
'Four days from now.'
'Do you have the cargo?'
'Sixteen girls and one lad.'
'Hmm… how much will you get for them?'
'4.000 coins[4] per girl and 5.000 coins[5] for the lad.'
'So… 69.000 Spanish Real[6] in total.'
'You will get your thirty percent… as promised…'
'So… 20.700 coins[7] for me and 48.300 coins[8] for you?'
'Correct!'
'Hmm… who is the buyer?'
'I rarely share such information… but it is a Scottish farmer who has ties to a company in Cornwall.'
'Hmm…. Those British…'
'In any case… I will arrive in Bermuda where I will transport them to the importer, and I will be paid there.'
'Will you continue further to Europe?'
'Likely I will… I will have the money when I get back.'
'Maybe we need to change plans… come back to Guatemala first… with the situation going on in Europe, there is a high risk your ship may be hijacked, and you will lose everything.'
'I was thinking about that too…'

---

[4] In today's money €25.500
[5] In today's money €31.875
[6] In today's money €439.375
[7] In today's money €131.962,50
[8] In today's money €307.912,50

‘By the way, I have a woman who wants to post some Mayan jewellery to some relatives in Britain.’
‘I can hand that over to the importer too if you prefer.’
‘Do that!’
‘The day after tomorrow I will come again with the last paperwork.’
‘That is good… you will depart from Trujillo?’
‘I will depart from Veracruz…’
‘How do you manage to do this?’
‘Bypassing Spanish customs is not easy, but if you have good connections in Mexico City, you can get away with it.’
‘I would never even try to do that… the punishments are high for violating Spanish customs… especially if you are a foreigner.’
‘You are no foreigner… they will favour you.’
‘In any case… there is something else.’
‘What?’
‘Fiona might become a problem for us.’
‘Well, then get rid of her.’
‘She is now involved with some Matagalpan thug…’
‘Hold on… Matagalpa? Those gangs do not play around, Carlo. You got to watch out with her then.’
‘She is pregnant of one of those guys.’
‘Dude...’
‘I know right…’
‘So, what do you plan to do about it?’
‘When you get back to Guatemala, come to the foundation immediately. We need to find a way to set her up… and her man… so they disappear.’
‘I never went so far… Carlo.’
‘Neither did I… but we might have to… if we want to save our own behinds.’
‘What did you do with that Mayan lady? I heard she had multiple knife wounds.’
‘Look, I do not even like to look at a blade… you know that of me. I have nothing to do with Marcella’s death.’
‘Well, it is not me you need to convince. People are talking about you…’
‘Talking?’

'Beware... Carlo. You either will get a whole mob of avenging Mayans after you... or the Captain General will get angry, and he will have you arrested.'
'I got this...'
'I hope you do!'
'Look, I need to go now. Meet me the day after tomorrow in night.'
'Got ya!'
Jacques-Marie left. Carlo went home.
The next day, the Royal Audiencia of Guatemala approved the arrest warrant for Fiona Rodrigues. The vice-Governor of the capital district sent ten auxiliary troops to go out and look for the suspect. The ten officers arrived at the foundation, but they did not find Fiona over there. Then the officers went to the places where she was often seen. She was not found over there also. Fiona, however, was asleep in a different room – in the foundation's building – when the officers came to arrest her. The next morning, her staff informed her that people came to arrest her.
'Oh dear...'
'Fiona, you need to get out of here!'
'What about the foundation?'
'Carlo can take over your duties as long as needed.'
'Good... then I will go with Rensy to Nicaragua for a while.'
'Do it as soon as possible...'
'I will do it during the night... when nobody expects it.'
'Where is Rensy?'
'He is at some pub getting drunk probably.'
'I will inform him. Stay inside till tonight!'
'I will!'
Carlo grabbed Rensy at the pub and he dragged him to the garden of the foundation.
'What the hell are you doing?'
'Carlo... yet need to man up!'
'Manning up...'
'Listen... you have a pregnant partner who is wanted by the authorities for a crime she did not commit. For the sake of your child and her, you need to make sure that she is safe!'
'I did not sign up for this...'
'The moment you decided to stick your cock in her pussy you signed up for all the risk that would come afterwards. BE A MAN!'

'She can stay with a nephew of mine… together with me… in Masaya.'
'You will go with her there tonight. You will also keep me updated, DAILY, about her condition. Understood?'
'Got it!'
'Now… get a shower and get yourself together. You look like crap!'
'Well, thank you for being so kind…'
Carlo walked away.
At that same moment, Jacques-Marie encountered a group of Oaxaca Indians that came after him. He had to run for kilometres before he was able to hide on an abandoned farm from the violent mob. He realised that the group likely found out about the sale of a 22-year-old Oaxacan woman to some German cartel, two months earlier. Jacques-Marie was the one overseeing the transfer. He was paid 900 Spanish Real[9] for his part.
That moment became an eye-opener to the French human trafficker: he wanted to stop. He decided that this transaction would be his last in the prostitute trafficking business. When he returned to the capital, he went to the French Embassy to inform them about his voyage to Bermuda. However, the French diplomats only took his written statement and they kicked him out of the chancery. Most of the French diplomats, in Spanish America, were not in favour of the current French Republic. Jacques-Marie, an open supporter of the French Revolution and the French Republic, gained a bad reputation throughout the French community in the Viceroyalty of New Spain. He was known as 'Jacques the butcher' by most French migrants. He attempted to date several French women, but all of them rejected him due to his support for the 'traitors' of Bourbon France.
When he left the chancery, he encountered several prostitutes on the street with whom he became carnal several times.
'Asshole!'
The women came after him. He still owed them money for their last sexual encounters. He ended up fleeing the capital that same hour.
At that same moment, Huyên knocked on Fiona's door. Fiona woke up from a deep sleep to answer her.
'Oh… it is you, Huyên. What is going on?'
Huyên pulled her out of the office.
'Huyên… what?'

[9] In today's money €5.737,50

The Vietnamese woman dragged her to a chariot, where Rensy was awaiting her.
'Rensy?'
'We need to get out of here! It is not safe!'
'I know… Carlo already informed me.'
'Then we have no time to waste.'
'I want Huyên to come with us.'
'What?'
'She is a good servant…'
'Look…'
'Either she comes with us… or we are not going.'
'Fine!'
Huyên jumped into the chariot with them, and they rode out of Guatemala City. Just several hours later, the chariot arrived at Santa Ana where the rider decided to lodge at a small inn. After arriving at the inn, Fiona walked towards the farm-estate of the Muriyamas. She arrived at the front door of the main building when one of the servants opened for her. The servant brought her to the living room where she was told to wait.
After several minutes, the wife of Taro Muriyama arrived.
'Fiona?'
'Minyeong!'
'Great to see you!'
'I am glad to be here too…'
'What brings you here?'
'I am on my way to Masaya…'
'Why?'
'Well, there is an arrest warrant on me.'
'What?'
'Those two politicians… for some reason they think I am involved.'
'That in nonsense… you know that.'
'In any case… I can end up in prison for years if they decide to convict me.'
'Your father will not allow that to come so far…'
'Well, I have not seen him taken any action yet.'
'I am sure he is active for you.'
'How is Taro?'
'He is fine… we are planning another trip to Korea.'
'That is great!'

‘It is time for me to see some of my relatives again.’
‘However, will you not get in trouble with the Japanese sailors when you pass near their shores?’
‘That depends.’
‘In any case, beware that you are not locked up by the Shogunate.’
‘Taro is Japanese... remember?’
‘A Japanese who serves the Spanish king… that is a big difference.’
‘In any case… we might depart within a month or two… we are not sure yet.’
‘At least you will have a better time there than me over here… I am officially a fugitive now.’
‘Remain in hiding until the case is resolved.’
‘That is what I plan to do… I just met this Vietnamese woman several days ago… she does not speak Spanish that well. Her father is a merchant that arrived here for trade.’
‘So, you got your new personal assistant?’
‘Yeah…’
‘Just beware.’
‘She barely speaks Spanish. She is not a threat to anyone.’
‘If you say so…’
‘I will message Brittany soon about my whereabouts.’
‘Do not do that!’
‘Whaa?’
‘Brittany and you are on good terms… but first, she is a foreigner and secondly, her loyalty is not to you… so, she will likely snitch on you when the authorities put pressure on her. You cannot be deported, she can. So… remember that!’
‘You are right.’
‘Brittany is not the type of individual to be involved in a matter like this.’
‘Got it!’
‘Apart from Brittany, have you heard anything about that case of that murdered Mayan woman?’
‘I heard about it… vaguely.’
‘According to Taro, she was assassinated to silence several Mestizo extortioners from Chimaltenango.’
‘Hmm…. I am not really aware of all the conflict in Guatemala.’
‘Well, you should… because you have become the centre of the conflict around here.’

‘The centre?’
‘The whole issue with your father’s income, the conflicts in your family, the murder of those two Spanish politicians and the escalating conflicts amongst the mestizo traders here in the north… all of this violence needs a centre figure as a point of release… and that has become you.’
‘Me?’
‘They will put the blame on you and focus on destroying you, that is what I see happening right now.’
‘Come on, Min…’
‘I am telling you, there is no reason why any courthouse should suspect you of a political double homicide… you can clearly see it is a setup, right?’
‘I do see that.’
‘Why would they set you up?’
‘As a distraction?’
‘Exactly! You are in an unbelievably bad position, Fiona. Realise that danger that you are in.’
‘So… staying in the south till the situation is resolved.’
‘Also, do not be active in the foundation until its over.’
‘Carlo has taken things over as the vice-President.’
‘Hmm… I do not trust him.’
‘Why not?’
‘Something about him feels off…’
‘Like?’
‘Look… the first time I saw Carlo, I felt as if I was being chocked. That man is not who he claims to be.’
‘I do remember seeing him talking to this French man often.’
‘What French man?’
‘There is this French captain that he often talks to… in French. I have no idea what they are discussing. I know French quite well… but they always seem to argue.’
‘Hmmm… I told you so.’
‘France is in a mess… so, I do not know what he wants to achieve.’
‘He might be using his job as a vice-President to cover up his criminal activities.’
‘Who does not have criminal income around here… this is the Kingdom of Guatemala we live in… not the Viceroyalty of Peru.’
‘Well, Carlo is an Italian… so, he might have double loyalties.’

'Double loyalty…'
'He might be here just to earn a lot of cash and then he moved to some place in Italy.'
'Italy is divided…a portion is still managed by Spain, while the rest are competing with each other.'
'That does not matter… He is Italian and he might feel more connected to them than to Spanish America… even though Italian Spaniards did contribute much to the Spanish economy.'
'Another thing I noticed about Carlo… is that I seldom see him with a woman.'
'Say that again?'
'I never saw him with a woman… in a sexual context.'
'Hmmm… that is a big red flag.'
'I know right… However, I kept my mouth shut because I did not want to cause any controversy.'
'He is a controversy… what if that French captain is his lover?'
'Come on… Min… that goes to far.'
'That might… but the fact that you see him often bitching with that Frenchman instead of caressing a woman speaks volumes.'
'True… but I always gave him the benefit of the doubt.'
'Sometimes you should not give people the benefit of the doubt… the fact that there is doubt about whether or not they are safe… should trigger an investigation.'
'The owners of the foundation are two families that reside in the Kingdom of Galicia, mainland Europe.'
'Old Galicia is a very old-fashioned society… I am even surprised that they were interested in Guatemala at all.'
'Sometimes, Min… I think that this whole Santa Barbara Foundation is a setup.'
'I was thinking the same… but we have no proof.'
'We have no proof indeed… but it is weird indeed that the owners of the foundation have none of their relatives to represent them… in their own business. That does feel like a red flag.'
'It is a red flag!'
'I never had contact with any of the owners of the foundation.'
'Look', Minyeong sat next to her, 'you being the President is not a crime… so nobody can hold you liable if the owners, who live across the Atlantic Ocean, are involved in some type of money laundering.

However, you should be aware that you are dealing with unreliable people.'
'I figured that out quickly!'
'There is something else you may not have noticed.'
'What is that?'
'Why is it that Vietnamese merchants suddenly get interest in Spanish America?'
'I am not following you?'
'The distance from the Viet Kingdom all the way to Guatemala is quite long and the sail route is extremely dangerous… so the safest way for them to sail is via Manila Galleon route. So, that begs the question… why do they not trade with the Spanish via Manila, which is closest to them?'
'Hmm… there may be some reason why they prefer to come to Spanish America by themselves.'
'All those societies in Asia pay tribute to the Chinese Emperor… to be able to participate in their trade… and the Chinese have a good deal with the Spanish Empire… that works out well for all Asians that seek to trade with the Americas… and now… you have Vietnamese people bypassing this great deal, which has been effective for centuries already… to come to a region that they do not know and which language they barely master?'
'Well, maybe they are curious…'
'Fiona, you have a good hearth… a good, soft, feminine heart… and I value that. However, in this world… especially as a woman… you need to be streetwise too!'
'Why do you think they are here?'
'They might want to participate in the smuggling business that happens in the Province of Nicaragua…'
'If they are caught, they are in big trouble.'
'If multitudes do it… they cannot catch the whole multitude.'
'That brings the question why Mister Yu, Huyên's father, came to Guatemala.'
'He is here to exploit… or he is a fugitive… like you.'
'Fugitive?'
'What better way to avoid prosecution in your homeland than by fleeing to a foreign empire across the Pacific Ocean?'
Fiona thought about what her Korean friend told her. She realised that Minyeong's thoughts were not unrealistic at all.

'You may be correct about this…'
'So, you are now in the company of his daughter. That is a good method to keep him in check. Just do not trust this Mister Nyu!'
'I will not…'
'By the way, when is Brittany's brother arriving?'
'How do you know he is coming?'
'She told me last time she was here…'
'Ah… I remember again. Well, if he left Britain on time… he should be here tomorrow or within three days.'
'Do you think her brother is handsome?'
'Well, based on the portraits drawn of him… I think so.'
'Well, he might be a better match for you than that Matagalpan thug that you are with now.'
'He is the father of my baby.'
'That does not mean you have to stay with him. I am telling you, Fiona, that man will either abandon you after the baby is born… of he will stay with you… but he will trouble and violate you for decades. It is better for you, as Spain's duchess, to get a better man.'
'A better man… you propose I marry a nobleman from Spain?'
'It does not have to be a nobleman across the ocean. It can also be a Zambo[10] chief…'
'Zambo chief? I kind of fancy that idea… I never thought about it before.'
'There are around sixty of them in the Province of Honduras alone… sixty chiefs that manage their villages and households without any interference of the Spanish government. That is an impressive accomplishment. Taro often visits them and some of them came here. As the vice-regal diplomat, Taro makes sure that there is harmony between them and the Royal Audiencia.'
'You should meet them once… there are some Zambo chiefs in Nicaragua too…'
'I will check it out soon.'

[10] Someone of both African and Amerindian descent.

6

Brittany's older brother, *Mike*, arrived in Trujillo on a British mail delivery ship. The journey from Dover to Trujillo lasted in total 49 days, because the ship also stopped at some other ports in the Caribbean. Mike was a security guard in the port of Dover, and he took Spanish classes past years. Mike agreed to visit his younger sister in Spanish America last year after sending some Christmas gifts to her.
Mike showed his documentation which permitted him to remain in Spanish America for a maximum of six months. He was not allowed to purchase land nor to participate in local politics. He was also due to pay taxes upon every business transaction he made. After receiving his papers back from the custom's officer, he called a chariot. His Spanish was quite good.
'Sir, where do you need to go?'
'Guatemala City.'
'That will take three days or maybe four days depending on the weather on the road. We will have to stop at local inns to spend the night. So, all together It will cost you 4 Spanish Real and 3 additional coins for potential extra costs.'
'So, 7 Spanish Real in total? I am fine with that!'
'You can hop in right now. Do you have the exact address where you have to be?'
'Just bring me to the British Chancery and from there I will figure out where to go.'
'All right.'
After jumping in, Mike wrote several pages in his diary. He also had some pemmican left from the journey. After three days, the chariot stopped at a small town named Jalapa for the night.
'We will continue in the early morning. Get some rest and a shower if you want.'
'I will, till tomorrow!'
The sun was already set, and the people of the town were mostly inside their homes. There were only some Spanish soldiers, here and there, and some merchants that transported their goods at this time. Mike entered the inn where the rider checked in for them both. In the inn, Mike ordered a small beer and he sat down to check some of the paintings on the walls. He was impressed by the high quality of the native painters.

He noticed one specific painting which was signed 'Fiona Rodrigues y de Olmeda, 1798'. He remembered that this was the name of Brittany's Spanish friend.
'Sir, this painting is made by a Spanish woman named Fiona?'
'Exactly! It was donated to us early in 1799. Miss Rodrigues is not the President of the Santa Barbara Foundation in Guatemala City.'
'Santa Barbara Foundation?'
'It is that foundation that looks after disadvantaged Mayan people.'
'Ah… I see.'
'You can visit her in the capital if you are on your way there.'
'I will think about it, thanks. Can I have another beer, please!"
'Sure!'
After receiving his beer, he checked around a little more before he went to the dorm to get some sleep. The next morning, just before sunrise, he woke up with a little hangover. He quickly got a cold shower before he jumped into the chariot. However, he waited for over an hour and the driver did not come. When he went to the receptionist, the receptionist told him that the driver checked out an hour after checking them both in.
'Where did he go?'
'I have no idea… he did not ask for his money back. He just wanted us to allow you to remain here for the night.'
'Thank you!'
Mike walked back to the chariot. He could not believe that a chariot rider would leave his horses and chariot behind like that. When he checked the rider's seat, he found a note written in English:

When you read this, GET OUT OF JALAPA IMMEDIATELY! I will get new horses and a new chariot soon anyway. JUST LEAVE!

Mike was conflicted by what he read, in perfect English. However, he did what the note stated, and he left towards Guatemala City. He was not an experienced rider, but he was experienced enough to guide the horses on the highway to the capital. He was right on time. Shortly after he left, several thugs from Trujillo arrived to kidnap him. However, the thugs did not find him anywhere. If Mike would have stayed in Jalapa for just ten more minutes, he would have been in big trouble. After just five hours, he arrived at Guatemala City. At arrival, it was already past midday and he longed to take some extra rest. When he passed with his

chariot through the city, he was looking for the British flag. Eventually, he found the British Chancery where he parked the chariot.
When he entered the British chancery, the receptionist recognised him immediately.
'Michael?'
'Ey… Andrew!'
'What brings you here?'
'I am here to visit my younger sibling, Brittany.'
'When did you arrive…'
'Five days ago… in Trujillo after weeks of sailing and being seasick.'
'Well, you are here now… it has been a while.'
'How long have you been serving here in Spanish America?'
'For five months. It pays well and Guatemala is a peaceful territory where no troubles occur against British folks easily.'
'Good to hear…'
'What do you need?'
'The chariot rider left me his two horses and chariot as a gift… I have no problem with that. However, I do not want to pay taxes for something I received, not purchased.'
'Do not worry… I will do some paperwork for you to get you off it.'
'Have you seen Brittany lately?'
'I saw her at the French bakery two days ago. She was together with Josephine.'
'I need to know their address…'
'We cannot just give that, Mike.'
'I am her brother… you know that is true.'
'Hmm… I will move some documents and then I will check something out. Come on…'
Andrew placed the address on display for Mike to read it.
'Thanks!'
'How long will you stay?'
'At least three months, I think. I have a permit for six months.'
'Well, stay out of Petén.'
'Why is that?'
'There are Indian revolts going on there… and some even kidnapped Spanish residents.'
'Oh gosh…'
'So, you can go anywhere… except the zones that have territorial disputes.'

‘That Spanish America still has territorial disputes with the Indians these days.’
‘The Mosquito Coast, Bocas del Toro and Peten. Those areas are not recommended for foreigners nor locals.’
‘I have no business going to the Mosquito Coast. We have been evicted from there since 1786…’
‘Mike… there is something you need to know.’
‘What is it?’
‘Brittany’s Spanish friend, Fiona, is a fugitive.’
‘Fugitive?’
‘She is being wanted for involvement in the double homicide of two Spanish politicians.’
‘Get out of here!’
‘It is true… and her father is also under investigation. However, her father lives all the way in Guayaquil. They might arrest him later also.’
‘Damn!’
‘I recommended Brittany to stay away from Fiona as long as she is not cleared by the court.’
‘Well done!’
‘But… Mike…’
‘There is more?’
‘Fiona is pregnant…’
‘Out of wedlock?’
‘Yes.’
‘That happens often.’
‘She was impregnated by a man from a Matagalpan gang.’
‘Hmm…. Is she out of her mind?’
‘She probably is.’
‘Then I was right after all… that Fiona appeared self-destructive, and she is exactly that. It is good that she is gone now and removed from Brittany.’
‘Do not get involved, Mike.’
‘I am here to see my sibling and to relax in the Spanish rainforests… that is it!’
‘I am glad we are on the same page.’
‘Anything else I should be warned about?’
‘Do not travel via Trujillo anymore! There are many violent mobs that seek to set up British and French migrants that arrive via that port. When you travel, travel via the other Spanish ports… or… as a

Briton… you can sail to British Honduras and you can continue from there. Trujillo is too dangerous!'
'Understood!'
Mike left the British Chancery and he walked towards the address that he saw on the notebook. At arrival, he knocked on the door. Then several seconds later, he heard his name.
'Michael!'
He turned around and his younger sibling embraced him.
'Brittany!'
'I am glad you made it!'
'Me too!'
'I will be cooking, Brit…', Josephine excused herself, 'Nice to see you again, Mike!'
When Josephine walked away, she noticed that there were two masked men approaching the building. She quickly got her gun out and she fired it at them. The burglars ran away. When she arrived in the kitchen, she began chopping the unions, garlic, peppers, and limes. While cooking, someone familiar walked in.
'Jo…'
'Hey Rodrigo!'
'What are you cooking?'
'Some rural mestizo dish I learned about several weeks ago.'
'Can I join?'
'Of course! How is your father?'
'He is doing well.'
'That is good!'
Rodrigo sat down.
'By the way, Brittany's brother is here.'
'That is good. She was really hoping to see him.'
'You heard about Fiona?'
'I did… as one of the first. I never believed any of those allegations.'
'The allegations are ridiculous.'
'There must be something up for them to frame her like this!'
'I think she knows too much.'
'Well, she or her father knows too much. I think it is her father.'
'Why do they not go after her father?'
'That is what they are doing… by targeting her, they know that the father will respond.'
'Ahh…. I get it!'

'Where is she now?'
'I have no idea… she left with that boyfriend of hers to some place in the south.'
'Of Guatemala?'
'Yeah… I am not sure whether it is in Nicaragua or Costa Rica… there are down there somewhere.'
'That is better… she needs to step back from public life for a while. I was never fond of her being so into the open. Being so into the open attracts enemies.'
'Hmm… sometimes I think that Brit's brother is attracting danger.'
'Why so?'
'When we came back from the market, we saw him knocking on the door. I walked away to give the siblings some time alone. When he was about to enter the building through another entrance, I saw two masked burglars… thank God I had my gun with me, and I scared them off.'
'That is nasty!'
'We never had this before… now that this British dude appears, we suddenly have trouble. It is not the first time. Everyday one of his letters arrived, we would encounter almost-accidents in the guesthouse. There is something off with that man.'
'He may be afflicted by generational curses.'
'Well, I just do not want his generational afflictions to afflict us.'
'Well, maybe you should consider that Brit might also have afflictions that haunt her.'
'She is fine…'
'Well, she is not. She has a lot of unresolved pain that she hides by working a lot. That is not healthy.'
'She does contribute to the community, though.'
'At her own long-term well-being? That is not correct, Josephine. You know better!'
'I also have my own issues… I just make sure others are not bothered by it.'
'Well, whether others are bothered by it or not is irrelevant. What is relevant is that the unresolved issue is there and sooner or later that issue will escalate. Do not think you are in control! You are not!'
'Thanks for the fatherly lessons, Rodrigo.'
'Where are the two British siblings now?'
'I have no idea… they will likely come here soon.'
'Then complete whatever you are cooking.'

'Where are you going?'
'I have szome business to take care of around here.'
'Will you come back?'
'Yeah…', he opened the door, 'I will… save some of the dish for me!'
'No problem!'
'¡Adios!'
When she completed cooking, Josephine went looking for Brittany and Mike. She did not find them anywhere. She was then suddenly grabbed by her neck and pushed into an ally.
'So, we finally meet… Miss Josephine the 'know it all!'
'Who the hell…'
'Do not tell me you forgot about me!'
It was Josephine's ex-boyfriend whom she reported for his violent escalations.
'Gerald… get out of here!'
'Or else what… you think I could not find you?'
'We are done, Gerald. Done!'
'Well, not before I teach you a lesson.'
'Well,', Josephine pulled her small gun and shot him in his foot, 'You asked for it!'
He fell to the ground due to the pain that shocked his body.
'You still want to mess around with me, Gerald?'
'You will be sorry about this!'
'The only one that will be sorry is you if you do not get your ass out of here! I have reserve bullets, you know?'
Gerald stumbled away. When he was out of sight, Josephine put her gun down. It was not the first time that he assaulted her like that.
Josephine walked back to the kitchen and there she saw Brittany serving the food to her elder brother.
'Jo!!'
'I see you are serving yourself already.'
'Of course, I am!'
'It is a mestizo stew, with Spanish salmon and come lobster.'
'Lobster is sweet!'
Brittany served food for Josephine too and all three ate at the same time. While eating, the mail delivery came with a post package for Josephine. She opened the letter that was written by her mother. Her mother informed here that her granduncle passed away and that an

inheritance of 300 British Pounds would be shipped to her as soon as possible.
She decided to keep the news to herself by pretending that it was just a long letter from her nosy mother. Back at the table, the three drank some plum juice together.
'The plum juice from here is far better than anyone I drank in Britain.'
'This is Spanish plum juice… of course it is superior.'
'The fruits are also grown in a tropical climate… that also plays a role.'
'Hmm… you think that is it?'
'Of course, Britain has a very cold climate… so fruits that grow there are different from fruits that grow in a tropical environment.'
'You may be right about that!'
While drinking an extra cup of plum juice, Brittany saw a woman approaching them.
'Ma'am, can we help you?'
'Yes', the woman wore expensive jewellery, 'I am looking for Fiona Rodrigues, my niece-in-law.'
'She is not here… you have to go to the Santa Barbara Foundation, which is located near the garrison. They might be able to help you further.'
'Thank you!'
The woman turned and left.
'Who was that?'
'I have no idea… probably the wife of one of Fiona's uncles.'
'She only has two paternal uncles… one lives in Cartagena de Indias and the other in Seville.'
'Even if that is the case, why is she here alone?'
'She seemed tired… as if she came from a long journey.'
'Whether she came from Cartagena de Indias, or all the way from Cadiz, she needs to go to the foundation to find out where Fiona is now.'
'She probably knows nothing about Fiona's arrest warrant.'
'We will also not tell her. It is not our place to.'
'I get you!'
'She wore expensive jewellery. So, I do not doubt whether she is related to Fiona or not… even if it is only through marriage.'
'She needs Fiona for something.'
'I wonder what…'
'Is that our concern?'

‘It, is’, Brittany began washing the dishes, ‘Fiona is a friend of ours and her well-being should concern us!’
‘All right… but she is a fugitive now.’
‘She did not break the law.’
‘I am not saying that she did…’
‘What are you saying?’
‘Things are not as usual now. We need to consider the scenario that we might not see Fiona ever again if this situation turns out ugly.’
‘Hmmm… that is something I do not want to think about.’
‘We will have to!’
‘Hold on… but should we not try to find out more about that woman?’
‘Well, let the foundation deal with it. Carlo is a strict vice-President. He will deal with her.’
What they were not aware off was that the woman never left, but she remained close to the door and she overheard their conversation. She ran away towards the foundation to find out whatever she could about Fiona’s whereabouts. When she arrived, Carlo was adamant in not telling her anything.
‘Look, I am the wife of Lionel Rodrigues!’
‘Yes, I know who you are…’, Carlo sat down, ‘and I am the vice-President of this prestigious foundation. I cannot inform you about the whereabouts of your niece-in-law without potentially endangering her.’
‘You can be arrested for obstruction of justice, you know?’
‘Nobody can proof that I know where she is…’
‘I can…’
‘Are you extorting me?’
‘I do know about your little export to Europe.’
‘What are you talking about?’
‘Do not play dumb, Carlo. You arrange the deportation of girls for prostitution. You have this French guy that helps you, right?’
‘What are you talking about?’
‘Maybe we should ask Jacques-Marie about it directly.’
‘Hold on’, Carlo stood up, ‘How do you know about Jacques-Marie?’
‘I got you!’
‘Look, what do you want?’
‘I want to visit Fiona.’
‘Your niece in law is being set-up for some type of political drama that is going on.’

'That is why I want to visit her. I might be able to help her. I sailed all the way from Spain just to meet her.'
'You crossed the whole damn ocean for Fiona?'
'Yeah…'
'She is not even your daughter. You are out of your mind.'
'That is reason enough for you to help me as soon as possible… before I rat you out!'
'Hold on', he wrote down the address on a note for her, 'Here you go!'
'That was not hard, was it?'
'Just keep me out of it!'
'I just did… now stay out!'
The woman left. Outside, the stepped into a chariot towards the address that Carlo gave her.
After she left, Brittany arrived at the foundation.
'Carlo!'
'What now?'
'You sound annoyed.'
'I am… I was just extorted into telling where Fiona was.'
'Was it her aunt-in-law?'
'Yeah… how do you know?'
'She came to our residence first… while we were eating.'
'What a degenerated creep is she!'
'Is she dangerous, you think?'
'Well, I do not just think it. I KNOW IT!'

7

Lionel's wife arrived in Masaya, where Fiona was hidden from the authorities. After asking the locals, she found the residence of Rensy's nephew where Fiona stayed together with Huyên. At arrival, she opened the door that was unlocked. She walked into the house, until she encountered a tanned Asian woman.
'Who are you?'
The Asian woman did not respond. Fiona arrived.
'Mathilde!'
'Fiona… that has been a while!'
'Five years to be exactly!'
'You have grown a lot!'
'I am a young woman now… I am not a child anymore.'
'I am glad I am here.'
'Where in Uncle Lionel?'
'He is in Seville…'
'You crossed the ocean without him?'
'I was on my way to visit an old friend in the Province of Oaxaca… however… the ship landed in Trujillo instead of Veracruz. I thought… why not visit my favourite niece in law before I continue to Oaxaca?'
'Well… I am glad you are here auntie… however… these are not the best times for me.'
'I heard that you are a fugitive.'
'Dad's political concerns are afflicting me now. It is nothing new.'
'I knew that your father would sooner or later get you involved in his mess…'
'It is my father… Gregorio. He is always like that.'
'In any case, I am here now…'
'Just know that this is not my home. It belongs to a relative of my boyfriend.'
'Boyfriend?'
'Yes, I am pregnant, and he arranged this place for me to hide.'
'Does your father know about this?'
'No. I have not informed him.'
'Do not inform him either. He will be upset that you become pregnant out of wedlock.'
'I know… I know.'

'Look, I will keep this a secret too… but that guy you are with… is he notable?'
'Well, he is from a chieftain's household…'
'A warlord, you mean…'
'Whatever, I am fond of him and he is fond of me.'
'Just beware!'
'Thanks for your concern, auntie!'
'By the way, who is this Asian woman?'
'She is my personal assistant. She barley speaks Spanish.'
'Then how do you communicate?'
'With hand sings and body language.'
'I wish I were able to do that!'
'It is not difficult.'
'So, how is life besides all of this.'
'Life is good here… I enjoy living in this kingdom. I prefer this place above Quito.'
'Quito is isolated at the Pacific.'
'Guatemala is connected to both North and South America and it connects both the Pacific and the Atlantic…'
'You really love this place.'
'I would like to spend the rest of my life here if I could.'
'Why would you not be able to do that?'
'Well, maybe… I do not know.'
'Do not try to figure the future out. Process the past and advance in the present.'
'Well said!'
At that moment, Rensy came home. Rensy was surprised to see three women in the living room speaking to one another.
'Hey, Rensy! This is my aunt-in-law, Mathilde!'
'Mathilde!'
'Rensy!'
'So, I will leave you both now… I and Huyên have some stuff to do. Bye!'
Huyên and Fiona left the house. It was warm weather and a clear sunny day.
'So, tell me… Rensy. What is your profession?'
'I do not have a profession, ma'am.'
'No profession? Then how do you make your income'.

‘I work as a mason’, Rensy felt quite uncomfortable with Mathilde’s attitude, ‘I work as a contractor.’
‘That is good. Then at least you have some way of supporting yourself and your family. When do you plan to have the wedding?’
‘Wedding?’
‘Marriage… when will you tie the knot.’
‘I have no idea, ma’am. Such are matters I discuss with Fiona alone.’
‘Hmm… what will her father say?’
‘I have never met her father.’
‘He might visit Guatemala soon. Are you ready to face his disapproval?’
‘Listen, woman… I do not appreciate you condescending on me like that in this place. It is only due to Fiona that I do not kick you out! I could not care less about your money nor your social rank. Nobody dishonours me in my own place.’
‘This is not even your own place. It belongs to a relative of yours.’
‘How do you…’
‘I have my ways of figuring things out. By the way, did your relative pay the required taxes?’
‘What?’
‘If he has tax liabilities… I will take care of that. Do not worry.’
‘Oh my God…’
‘Be of good cheer, young man. I am on Fiona’s side… and that includes you… for now.’
‘Mathilde, what is the real reason you are here?’
‘What?’
‘You crossed the Atlantic Ocean. That is a trip of roughly three weeks to a full month. You arrived here without your husband. Why did you do that?’
‘What is that to you?’
‘It seems to me that you wanted to flee your troublesome marriage.’
‘What do you know about marriage?’
‘I know how to recognise people who are hiding something. You, Mathilde, are hiding a secret and you want to keep something from your environment. That is the only way I can explain this voyage of yours. Do not pretend as if this is all for charity on the behalf of Fiona. You got an agenda and before I know it… I will figure you out.’
‘Do your best, young man.’
‘Be ready to be exposed once I figure you out… Ma’am!’

Mathilde left the building, and she went to one of the fountains in Masaya. There at the fountain, she saw how Fiona and Huyên were conversing with some of the locals. At that same moment, she decided to go back inside and to swallow her pride.
At some point, Huyên noticed three young men staring at them. She pulled Fiona's arm and Fiona also noticed it. The two ended their conversation with the locals and they walked away. Huyên led Fiona into an alley, where they escaped the sight of the three stalkers.
'Who are those creeps?'
The two women hid inside a chariot until they saw that the three stalkers left the street. Huyên noticed a map on the floor of the chariot. She handed it to Fiona. It was a map of Central America picturing the kingdoms Guatemala, Yucatan, and the duchies of Veraguas and Panama. She noticed that there were red dots on the map.
'What are these? I see there is one here in Masaya, two in Costa Rica and one in Panama.'
While she checked the map, Huyên saw some people walking towards the chariot. Huyên pulled her out of the chariot and the two hid in the alley right on time. Fiona still held the map though. The chariot rode away.
'Hmm… I still got the map, Huyên. I am curious to find out what those red dots are all about.'
The two walked back to the flat, where Rensy was awaiting them.
'Where have you two been?'
'We were just chatting around in town…'
'For so long?'
'Look… we were followed at some point, so we hid in a chariot.'
'By whom?'
'Just three weird looking men.'
'Oh... Lord…'
'We are still alive, Rensy!'
'That is not the point. We came here because it was safe.'
'Look', she showed him the map, 'I found this in the chariot.'
Rensy checked the map.
'This is a military map. It points out hidden military bases.'
'What?'
'You got this from a chariot?'
'Yeah…'
'Was the chariot decorated with the coat of arms of Guatemala City?'

‘Nah…’
‘Then that is suspicious. Anyway, come inside!’
Inside all three sat in the living room. Rensy took a better look at the map. He saw that the map was pressed in Mexico City in 1798.’
‘This is a relatively new map… so, whatever is in those hidden military bases must be quite important.’
‘What do you think is there?’
‘Military equipment, I guess. Guatemala is a well-guarded kingdom of the Spanish Crown, so I guess hidden military hotspots is their way of doing it.’
‘There are some of them in Panama too…’
‘Well, the military in Guatemala also guards Panama… but for diplomatic reasons, Spain removed Veraguas and Panama form the jurisdiction of Guatemala City.’
‘It would have been better if the whole of Central America was governed from Guatemala City…’
‘I get you’, he smiled when he heard her comment, ‘but in politics, you need to concede to prevent others from becoming upset.’
‘Who would become upset if Panama were under Guatemala’s jurisdiction?’
‘Well, Panama is where all the export from South America, except Venezuela and the ports at the Caribbean, is transferred, through the lakes, towards the Caribbean shores. In case of smuggling, the Royal Audiencia of Guatemala would detect is quickly… furthermore, it would make the Viceroyalty of Peru, which is considered of high rank, subjected to the customs of a lesser Spanish territory… so, to keep those in Peru happy, Panama and Veraguas remained part of Peru, until 1739.’
‘Hmm… interesting.’
‘You should know all of this.’
‘I knew some stuff about it… but not the deep reasons behind the history.’
‘It is always fun to learn something new.’
‘Well, I do not think we can do much with this map.’
‘Maybe you can check out what it is.’
‘Are you out of your mind?’
‘Whoa?’
‘Visiting a secret military base? You want me to be executed?’
‘Just check it out.’

‘Drop the idea… Fiona.’
‘Come on, darling. I am really curious.’
‘WHY?’
‘I think we might find some interesting stuff over there.’
‘Like what?’
‘Hidden treasures… the secret plans of our king… whatever.’
‘Secret plans?’
‘I am simply curious what our leaders are up to.’
‘We are governed by an aristocratic feudal empire… good luck with that.’
‘There must be some way to figure out…’
‘So, you want me to raid the hidden military bases?’
‘You can do it with others…’
‘I will think about it if you promise to stay inside until our baby is born.’
‘Deal!’
‘Good’, he stood up, ‘Huyên can go outside and do whatever outside chores you should do.’
‘Got it!’
‘By the way, keep your mouth shut against that aunt-in-law of yours. She is spooky and I feel she has bad intentions.’
‘I want her out…’
‘Then that will happen!’
That same night, Mathilde relocated to a small inn. She was upset, but she adapted quickly, nevertheless.
‘Happy?’
‘Yeah… now there is more peace in this house.’
‘I agree!’
‘Rensy… what if those men following us were send by the court?’
‘To arrest you?’
‘Yeah.’
‘If that were the case, they would have arrested you by now.’
‘Right!’
‘Nicaragua is a very sparsely populated province. We have around maybe 150 thousand people living down here… that is the Mosquito Indians not included. There is smuggling happening here… but not in Masaya. Besides that, there is bigger crime happening in the north… so, Nicaragua is the last place they would look for a fugitive.’
‘And… a portion of the Province is in rebellion against Spanish rule.’

'True!'
'How does your family cope with this?'
'Matagalpan people just remain low key… that is it.'
'I need to do that too…'
'Are you not?'
'Nope… I have been showing off myself too much.'
'You love the attention.'
'That is how we met!'
'Yet…'
'I know… it is not handy.'
Rensy suddenly realised something.
'Hold on… Fiona.'
'What?'
'This situation is a bit weird…'
'Tell me!'
'Your aunt-in-law crosses the Atlantic to see you… a Spanish court makes you the suspect in a case that you were not involved in…'
'Yeah?'
'I get the feeling that Mathilde is in on this situation.'
'How can she be in on it?'
'She is a peninsulares… she is more aware of politics than we are. What if she knows the truth behind the killed Spanish politicians? What if she knows that they were about to set you up?'
'Then why did she cross over to see me?'
'Maybe she is part of the plot… I do not know.'
'You are making wild speculations!'
'The whole situation around you is suspicious. Someone, somewhere, wants YOU to be the scapegoat.'
'I know that…'
'Then you must consider that maybe your own family is in on it.'
'Well, I might consider Uncle Lionel of being involved. He conflicted with the rest of the family who moved to South America. Lionel wants everything to centre around the policies of Seville and Cadiz, the two Spanish ports that manage Spanish America. My father, and my other uncle, wanted the focus to be on the improvement of the infrastructure in South America to boost the local economy…'
'I am not making wild guesses here… whoever set you up, is someone close.'
'That is a scary thought.'

'It is a realistic thought we should consider.'
'80% of all my relatives live in Spain, the other 20% is divided between Guayaquil and Cartagena de Indias.'
'So, that is reasonable of your uncle to remain focussed on Seville and Cadiz.'
'However, most of our income comes from South America, so it does not add up that Uncle Lionel does not want the local economies in South America to improve.'
'Uncle Lionel might not want the South American economies to become so strong that locals develop desire for independence.'
'That might be true…'
'It is simple… if the people in New Granada become so self-sufficient that they can operate freely without Spanish viceroys, then why should they not declare independence and start their own nation? Your uncle is realistic.'
'I never thought about it that way.'
'I think that is the reason why Panama was not made into a separate kingdom, as it should have been.'
'I get you!'
'But if we consider that your family is mainly living in Spain and that they depend on their relatives who live in South America, then it is understandable that this scandal surrounding your father is BAD NEWS to them.'
'So, my relatives have set me up to save their income?'
'That is what the evidence points to.'
'What other explanation can there be?'
'I have no other than the idea that maybe some locals, in South America, might have pressured your father to disown you… so the blame might fall on you.'
'Why would locals want that?'
'It is bad news for the local economy, which is already fragile, to be associates with a man suspected of treason.'
'Got it!'
'Fiona, your family has turned on YOU. Realise that!'
'It is something that I have difficulty to accept.'
'Well, you did the right thing by wanting Aunt Mathilde out of here. She seems nothing but an agent to me.'
'I do remember one time my father suggested splitting the family, so he could take over the 'South American branch'.'

'Splitting the family?'
'Yes', she walked towards the window, 'that would mean that our ties to the Iberian Peninsula would be broken and we would remain focussed only on Spanish America.'
'Why did he not do it?'
'Many of the business partners and investors of my father did not want to lose their connection to Europe… and New Granada being a Spanish viceroyalty implies that it would be financial suicide to cut off your connection to Seville and Cadiz.'
'So, as far as I can see… there is deep-rooted resentment within your family.'
'I guess… you can say that.'
'In that case… you should be happy that you are not living with your parents, nor with your other relatives… that might be the reason you are still alive.'
'Well, this all means I am like an orphan… right?'
'Not an orphan. You have people in this place that love you and who embrace you.'
'For how long? When my presidency is over… they are likely to forget all about me.'
'Not if you make yourself so relevant that they have to keep on thinking about you.'
'In that case… us finding that map might be a blessing in disguise.'
'Let us say, hypothetically, that we figure out some secret plot by the government… what will you do?'
'I will use the data to blackmail the viceroy to cancel the prosecution towards me… as well as to leave my father alone.'
'In that case, you will have to blackmail two viceroys.'
'If needed, I will do exactly that!'
'You are a bit too overconfident here… you, a simple woman, will blackmail military men?'
'I might do it covertly.'
'You are getting yourself into a lot of trouble… you are already haunted as a scapegoat and now you want to play politics with them?'
'Well, I am involved anyway… So, I might as well take my best shot at it!'
'Think about what might go wrong…'

'Think about what might go right. I might be able to clear my father's name, ease the family conflict and move on living a lovely family life with you by my side! That is what I long for!'
'Me too!'
'Good.'
'For us to be able to live a comfortable family life… we need to get away from all this drama. There is no way I see myself raising a child with all of that politics haunting me.'
'Then help me out… figure out what they are hiding at those bases. Then we can live like commoners… at peace!'
That same day, despite realising better, Fiona requested help from her father, and Uncle Lionel, concerning the situation she was in. One letter was sent to Seville and the other one to Guayaquil. The letter to Guayaquil arrived just eight days later. By now, Victor and Amadeo II were in Amadeo II's palace to discuss family matters. The arrival of the letter was an emotional moment.
'You see that Victor? Those creeps are setting Fiona up to get to me.'
'I know, brother. I know.'
'I am not allowing this to happen!'
'What are you doing?'
'I am writing a statement.'
'Hold on', he held his brother's arm, 'what type of statement?'
'Nobody will make my daughter the scapegoat of the failure of the Spanish authorities. I am a loyalist to Charles IV… but this goes way too far!'
'Remain calm!'
'I cannot remain calm as long as my daughter is fugitive. That is nothing for a woman!'
'I admit… you are correct!'
Victor and Amadeo II sent a letter to the court of Guadalajara demanding a dismissal of the case that afflicted Fiona. The letter arrived eleven days later in the postal box of the court of Guadalajara. The letter was well-received by the court of Guadalajara and a sign that their trap worked. However, the president of the court did not withdraw the arrest warrant – because he wanted to use the fright of being caught as a tool to stir Fiona in the direction I wanted. The judicial officers did not agree with the President's decision – most complied nevertheless out of loyalty to the Spanish legal system.
However, other trouble was already growing for Fiona…

8

Brittany and Josephine discovered the body of the two Chinese women just outside of the building of the Santa Barbara Foundation. The two women were called by their Spanish nicknames Filipa and Philippine. The two British ladies reported the corpses immediately and the authorities send officers to seal off the crime scene and to deal with the corpses. The next day, the French Embassy confiscated the belongings of the deceased women (with permission of the Royal Audiencia) – who were also the wives of French migrants. The two husbands, however, were nowhere to be found. Meanwhile, Jacques-Marie received an eviction notice of the Royal Audiencia of Guatemala: he was banned for a period of five years from entering the Kingdom of Guatemala. He could face up to five year in prison if he would re-enter their jurisdiction and a fine of 2.000 Spanish Real. Since Jacques-Marie already had many enemies in both Mexico City and Guatemala City, he decided to leave the continent for a while. The day after Jacques-Marie left Spanish America, by this time, Brittany already figured out who he was and that he was doing dirty business with Carlo. She followed him all the way to the ship that he departed to Spain with.
The next day, Brittany broke into Jacques-Marie former residency to figure out what type of man he truly was. The residency was in Trujillo and it was nothing but a small house near a lake.
Behind the scenes, Amadeo II's effort worked: The Royal Audiencia of Guatemala stopped its inquiry towards Fiona Rodrigue after receiving contradictive evidence about Fiona's alleged involvement in the crimes she was accused of. However, for some odd reason the Royal Audiencia did not inform anyone outside of its institutions about this development – not even Fiona's father who pleaded on behalf of his daughter.
Brittany spent the night in Jacques-Marie's former residence. The next morning, she noticed a bitter stench coming from the kitchen. She checked and found pork meat in a state of decay. She puked and she ran to the front door. When she was about to leave, she suddenly heard a cry for help.
'Hello?'
'Help me…. HELP!'
'Where are you?'
'Over here! Behind the wardrobe!'
'Hold on!'

She checked and there she found a copper-skinned woman that was tied behind the wardrobe. She untied her swiftly.
'How long have you been here?'
'I believe four days!'
'Who did this to you?'
'The criollos from San Pedro Sula. I was supposed to be sold to some French speaking brothel… but for some reason, the handler forgot about me.'
'Who is the handler?'
'I believe a man named Jacques…'
'Ah…', Brittany offered the survivor some water, 'we need to get out of here!'
When the two were outside, Brittany noticed that many of the residencies around appeared empty.
'This neighbourhood is used as a cover-up: there are no real people living here. This is where criollos bypass Spain's strict regulation by storing smuggled goods as well as enslaved people.'
'Hmm….'
'I want to go back to my family.'
'San Pedro Sula, right?'
'Correct!'
'Then we will go there!'
The two entered a chariot and Brittany paid the fare towards San Pedro Sula, where the two arrived two days later. At arrival, the survivor (whose name was Paula) knocked on her parent's door. Her parents were glad to see her.
'Daughter!'
'Mum! Dad! I am glad I am here! The Paz Brothers kidnapped me… I heard them talking to some French speaking man… I was about to be shipped to France… However, for some reason… this Jacques forgot me in the wardrobe where I was locked. Thank God this woman appeared.'
'I knew the Paz Brothers were bad news…'
'Keep it quiet that I am here… I do not want to be kidnapped again.'
'Do not worry, we will keep this quiet.'
Brittany looked around the house and she concluded that the family was not that well off. She left the parents with their daughter and she walked towards the local church. At the church, she fell asleep for two hours.

When she woke up, due to the loud prayers, she went to a local tavern to get some dinner.
At the tavern, she – to her biggest surprise – saw Rensy talking to some other men.
'Rensy?'
'Whooaa…', he was surprised, 'You?'
'We need to talk!'
Rensy excused himself and he sat at a separate table with Brittany.
'Brittany… what are you doing here?'
'I was following a suspicious man all the way to Trujillo.'
'Why would you do that?'
'I suspected him of human trafficking…'
'Well, we have slavery… you know.'
'Not slavery… sex trafficking.'
'Hmm…. What did you discover?'
'Not much… only that his name is Jacques-Marie Toulon and that he has likely departed from Guatemala by now.'
'All the effort… for nothing?'
'Not exactly', she made eye-contact, 'I found a girl in his wardrobe… whom he was about to ship to some brothel in France.'
'My God…'
'She is safe now.'
'Where is she?'
'I brought her to her parents…', she looked around her, 'I believe her name is Paula.'
'Ahh…'
'You know her?'
'I knew her uncle… Gabino… who was an associate of mine.'
'What happened to this Gabino?'
'He got shot a year ago… it was a broken armistice between two households.'
'Oh dear…'
'Well, such things happen in the streets.'
'I see a lot of weird things in the streets too…'
'What kind of weird things?'
'The building next to the foundation.'
'What is up with it?'
'I saw people burying a body in there.'
'What is in that building?'

'I believe the Royal Chamber of Commerce?'
'Hmm... if that is true... then blood money is part of this economy.'
'Is blood money not part of every economy. Think about all the enslaved Africans that die yearly while being transported to the Caribbean!'
'I know... I know...'
'There is one thing I am so proud of my country... slavery is abolished in Britain and they want to abolish it in their colonies too. I hope they put pressure on Spain to abolish slavery in Spanish America also.'
'Well, there might be a civil war throughout Spanish America before slavery is abolished. A lot of criollos depend on slave labour for their income. Especially in places as Costa Rica and Panama.'
'Well, that is why I chose to live in the north of Guatemala!'
'Hmm...'
'Besides that, there is something else I have noticed about Fiona.'
'What is it?'
'She always brings trouble wherever she goes.'
'Come on...'
'Rensy... think about it! When she arrived in Matagalpa... it led to a shooting. When she arrived in Leon, it led to multiple arrests. When she returned to the capital, it led to her almost getting arrested. She brings bad luck.'
'That is not a polite thing to say.'
'Sometimes being polite is not the best policy!'
'Look...'
Suddenly, Brittany pushed both down when a group of men entered the tavern. The men were armed.
'What?!'
'I think this is a robbery!'
'Come!'
The two sneaked away into the inner garden of the tavern, while they observed – from the bushes – what was unfolding.
The armed men, five in total, handed over a bag with money to the tavern owner.
'Did you succeed?'
'Yes, Sir. The Frenchman is out of the country.'
'What about the girl?'
'She was nowhere to be found in the flat. The harbour master confirmed that Mister Toulon departed to France several days ago.'

‘Well, that means that our interests here are safe’, the tavern owner counted the money, ‘That means business is going well.’
‘There might be an obstacle for us.’
‘What is it?’
‘There is a woman, in Guatemala City, who might be on us.’
‘A woman is a threat to our trade?’
‘She is from the Rodrigues Household.’
‘Rodrigues?’
‘She is the daughter of Gregorio Rodrigues.’
‘Is that not that duke who is suspected of killing two peninsulares?’
‘That is him right.’
‘Why is she a threat?’
‘Her Vice-President of the Santa Barbara Foundation warned Toulon that Fiona might be unto the trade.’
‘Then we pay her hush money.’
‘You do not understand, Diego. This woman is a political sensitive figure. She attracts to much attention.’
‘Then we get rid of her… easy!’
‘How do you plan to do that?’
‘We put her three metres under… simple!’
‘Sir…’
‘If she is a threat to his transport, she is finished. Or… we kidnap her, and we require a big ransom from her father. One of the two.’
‘There is another obstacle.’
‘What is that?’
‘Toulon, due to his other criminal escapades, has been banned from entering the Kingdom of Guatemala.’
‘For how long?’
‘At least five years…’
‘Oh Gosh…’
‘We can shift towards importing Brazilian girls instead.’
‘Then we have to bypass the Portuguese customs and those guys are a pain in the ass.’
‘For now, our export to France is over…’
‘Not if we find a replacement for Toulon.’
‘Where do we get a replacement all the way in Europe?’
‘I will work on that!’

‘Work on it as soon as possible. Our money lenders are waiting for their repayments and when they do not get their money by next year… some of our relatives will lose some limbs…’
‘Fear not… We got this!’
‘One more thing… we need to get rid of that annoying diplomat.’
‘Who?’
‘Taro Muriyama… or Taro Santiago de Vallerido y Muriyama…’
‘I know who that scumbag is…’
‘Well, he is on our ass!’
‘It will take a while before he figures us out!’
‘He has figured out over twenty-five criminal groups and he bankrupted many pirates past decade! That man is good in what he is doing.’
‘We should learn from him. He is dedicated to serve the flag of Spain and he does it with fierce dedication.’
‘We may need to remove him from the land of the living.’
‘Hold on!’
‘There is no other choice. We either have the money lenders on our ass or Taro is coming to smack us around.’
‘So, you prefer the money lenders?’
‘The money lenders serve some good purpose for us and we can blackmail them into restraining their violence. Taro we cannot restrain. We have nothing on him.’
‘We will deal with Taro later… now we need to find a gap for our income!’
‘Who is the one behind the ban of Jacques-Marie?’
‘How should I know…’
‘We have to pay him a visit to deal with him.’
‘Probably some military officer or some minister appointed by the viceroy.’
‘We will go on it… for now… I want some peace this afternoon.’
The criminals walked away, and the two youngsters remained shocked in the bushes.
‘Did you hear that?’
‘Yeah, Brit…’
‘That makes me thing about many of the spooky figures I have seen in the capital.’
‘What are you up to?’
‘What are YOU up to?’
‘I do not follow you…’

'What are you going to do about what you just found out?'
'What do you expect me to do about it?'
'At least something!'
'Let me think!'
'Think fast!'
After ruminating for several minutes, Rensy got an idea.
'Brit… I have a map… that Fiona found in a chariot.'
'She stole it?'
'She FOUND it!'
'Whatever…'
'The map contains hidden military barracks…'
'What is your plan?'
'We will go there to find out if there is something, we can use against the royal governors…'
'Wait…'
'We do that, and we then force the military to get involved in this matter.'
'Well, that is better than nothing!'
'Come!'
The two youngsters took two horses, and they rode all the way to the hidden barracks in the Province of Nicaragua. When the two arrived, the barracks was in a cave, near a native village.
The natives were dark skinned and kind towards them. One of the grandmothers even invited the two for dinner – an invitation they took.
After eating dinner, the two youngsters moved towards the cave.
'What do you hope to find here?'
'There is only one way to find out', he lit his lantern, 'Turn on your light!'
'Hold on!', Brittany put her oil lamp on, 'Got it!'
'Come!'
The two walked into the cave until they encountered several doors. When going through one door, they entered a tunnel which led to the other side of the hillside. There, there was a sealed off property with high fences with several cabins in it. There was two poles wit the Spanish flag on it and there was also a big Mary Statue. The sun did not set yet, so it was still light outside. Brittany entered one of the cabins, which was not locked. The cabin contained many herbs, medicines, as well as French books on native linguistics. The books were published in France in the mid-1790s.

'Did you find anything?'
'No…', Brittany showed him one of the books, 'Just some literature on medicine and native languages.'
'I have noticed one thing about the Spaniards…'
'And that is?'
'They love French!'
'It is one of the most popular languages that exist.'
'I ask myself why… it sounds so… feminine.'
'Do not say that to native French people!'
'It is the truth though!'
'Well, then you have not heard English yet… we even use softer sounds!'
'I heard you speak English…'
'Ah… true!'
'In any case, I do not think there is much we will find…'
'QUIET!'.
She put her hand on his mouth. Both turn around and they hear soldiers coming. Rensy closes the cabin as soon as possible and they hid under the bed. Right on time… because two soldiers entered in. The men spoke Galician Spanish.
'Caleb… what will you do with your wage?'
'What I always do… I will go to San Salvador to get some good booty…'
'That is all?'
'What else can I do over here?'
'I know San Salvador allows many vices that are abominable in other parts of the Spanish Empire… but maybe you can decide to invest a little.'
'In what?'
'There are Chinese goods coming in Acajutla two weeks from now. Those are the leftovers of a Manila Galleon fleet that were not sold in Mexico.'
'Hmmm…. what will an investment bring me?'
'Revenue… the Chinese need to have investments in ships to transport their goods illegally to Guatemala.'
'There is legal trade in the Province of San Salvador…'
'Well, it is really a grey market over there. Ships can arrive… but officially… the Kingdom of Guatemala is not entitled, by law, to trade directly with the Asians.'

'So, our leaders made a loophole to take advantage of… that is good."
'You only pay a small fee, and you are entitled to a portion of the profit.'
'What is the smallest fee?'
'50 Spanish Real.'
'And that entitles me too?'
'0,5% of the profit.'
'So, if a Chinese vessel makes a profit of 600.000 Spanish Real[11]… I will be paid 3.000 Real?'
'Correct!'
'Chinese ships sometimes even make 1.000.000 Spanish Real[12] after one journey on the Pacific. I am in on it! I want to invest 300 Spanish Real.'
'Do not become greedy…'
'It is not greed… I want to have an additional income besides the wage King Charles is paying us. I think we should be paid more of the dirty work we do for the Crown over here.'
'If you were stationed in South America, your wage would be triple the amount you earn now.'
'Yes, but South America has the hardest routes and the most difficult tasks!'
'Indeed!'
'Guatemala is an easy place to travel through…'
'I would say, the easiest within the whole empire.'
'So, when can I make my investment?'
'You can do it the day after tomorrow. Do not invest more than 100 Spanish Real, trust me.'
'Fine… I want to be able to earn a few thousand coins each half year. So, I am in on it!'
'You can save some money for when you go back home.'
'Well, I am not sure if I want to return to Galicia.'
'Why not?'
'Look, Santiago de Compostela and La Coruña are modern cities. However, the cities in Spanish America are better maintained than the cities in our homeland.'
'Spain benefits more from its overseas kingdoms than from the Iberian kingdoms…'

[11] In today's money €3.825.000

[12] In today's money €6.375.000

'That explains it… however, as a Galician Spaniard… I prefer to live outside of Galicia.'
'Well, your parents will be disappointed.'
'I am disappointed in them anyway, so… I do not care about what they feel about me.'
'Come on… you need to forgive them.'
'I know', he sat down on the bed, 'but not now… the wounds are still fresh.'
'So, you joined the Spanish Navy to flee from your abusive parents?'
'Yeah… I thought I was open about that.'
'I do not know man…'
'Look, I know we are told to honour our father and mother… but we are also told to stay away from evil. My parents are just evil… that is it. I do not want them near me. I prefer to be here, in Guatemala, working my ass off… in hard labour… then to be in the so-called comfort of my parental home.'
'I get now why you do not want to go back to Galicia.'
'Look, I will go back to Spain… Galicia is part of Spain. Spain has more kingdoms… It has Valencia, Murcia, Granada, Seville, Jaén, you name it… I am not bound to have to go to Galicia.'
'True!'
'Where will you go?'
'I will visit La Coruña to see my aunt and my mother. Afterwards, I will likely move to Portugal.'
'Why?'
'Portugal has more money and the people there are warmer. Galicia is a bit impoverished.'
'Except our cities.'
'I am a city guy… but I also prefer some peace of the rural areas.'
'Then Portugal is excellent for you!'
'I have a cousin that married a Portuguese woman from Oporto.'
'Oporto is still used as an important port to export to the United States.'
'All the Portuguese ports, on the Iberian Peninsula, are Spanish ports in disguise.'
'No doubt about that!'
'Look, I let us get some rest… we need to wake up early tomorrow!'
'Right!'
The other soldier left the cabin and the cabin resident fell asleep quickly.

9

Caleb, the Galician fighter, woke up after noticing that someone closed the door of his cabin. He checked outside quickly to see who it was that touched his door. He did not find anyone. He went back inside to sleep. He noticed that some of his belongings under his bed were moved. He suspected unlawful entry. However, he was so tired that he just fell asleep again.

Meanwhile, Rensy and Brittany were in an office going through documents. The documents were signed by a general that had a supervisory role of the military functioning of the Province of Nicaragua on behalf of the Council of the Indies. Spain often sends its commissioners to Spanish America to examine the well-functioning of Spain's constituent countries.

Brittany went through a document concerning the disappearance of five British sailors who were engaged with mestizas from León.

'Look at this!'

'What?'

'Five British sailors, who were stationed in the Mosquito Coast in 1783, disappeared just several days before the Treaty of Paris of 1784 was confirmed by the Royal Audiencia of Guatemala City. The five men vanished, and nobody found them anymore.'

'Let me check...'

Commissioner Philemon Pontes y Santos, on behalf of His Catholic Majesty, Charles III, King of Spain, and the Indies, inspected the criminal courts of the Province of Nicaragua, which became the new Intendency of Léon. Commissioner Pontes found out that the criminal courts neglected in their investigation to the five missing British sailors. The Commissioner, in agreement with the Royal Audiencia of Guatemala, decided to hide the case from the public to prevent social unrest. Furthermore, the hiding of the case was also to hide potential foul play from Matagalpan warlords who are still opposing Spanish rule in the Captaincy General of Guatemala.

'Matagalpan warlords?'

'That sounds like relatives of yours?'

'Likely...'

'Do you know anything about this?'

'1783 is a long time ago...'

'Still, five sailors, especially British sailors, do not just disappear that way.'
'This commissioner covered up what happened to those five men.'
'I think there are more things being covered up, look at this...'

On the 5th of February 1795, colonel Ramirez paid a sum of 12.400 Spanish Dollars[13] to the Province of Nicaragua to compensate for the farmers who partook in the illegal export to Scandinavia. The sixteen farmers were released from detention and their prison sentences abolished by the Captain General.

'It seems like the military is covering up a lot of stuff around here!'
'Check this out!'

On the 15th of August 1798, the court of San Salvador ordered Count Amadeo II of the Amatique Estate, in the Viceroyalty of New Granada, to give up all his commercial activities in the Captaincy General of Guatemala due to bribery of custom officers in Trujillo as well as the possible assassination of a Black athlete who worked on a local plantation.'

'Hold on!'
'Let us read that again...'
'It says... the possible assassination of a Black Athlete...'
'So, it is not proven that he did it.'
'No, apparently not.'
'So, Fiona's father is likely an assassin.'
'Or he made others do the work for him.'
'In any case, he was suspected of assassinating someone. It is weird that nobody looked further in this case.'
'The report was singed by Commissioner Pontes.'
'It seems to me that his Pontes has a career of supervising Guatemala...'
'That is not a surprise...'
Brittany thought for a moment.
'Rensy... you know what this means?'
'What?'
'That Fiona's presence in Guatemala might not be of her free volution as she claims. She might have been manipulated to live in this country by her relatives. Just think about it... she is from a wealthy household that lives in Seville, Cartagena de Indias and Guayaquil. Those are three

[13] In today's money €632.400

high quality Spanish urban areas to live in. Why would she want to live in Guatemala which is considered a periphery by most Spanish officials?'
'Hmm… that is odd indeed!'
'Guatemala has several places where there is open rebellion against the Crown… kidnappings as well as political murders happen around here. So, why would she… a criolla… want to dwell around her so freely? Think about it!'
'Furthermore, her aunt-in-law just arrived here.'
'That also… why?! For God's sake, why?!'
'I agree with you… the Rodrigues Household is up to something and Fiona is being used as a tool to distract the public.'
'Whatever they are plotting must be of significance…'
'Oh, check this out!'

The Viceroyalty of the Kingdom of New Granada has prohibited all shipments of Jacuqes-Marie Toulon under the suspicion of involvement in sex trafficking of native women to French brothels to Saint-Dominigue and mainland France. The ban will remain till the 1st of January 1801, as agreed by the judge in Santa Fé de Bogota on the 15th of August 1799. If Jacques-Marie Toulon sets foot on the territory of Viceroyalty of the Kingdom of New Granada, he will be imprisoned for five years and afterwards deported to France. The same will apply for the jurisdiction of the Captaincy General of Venezuela.

'Hmm….'
'I think we are on to something here.'
'Hmm… it seems like this Jacques-Marie is being kicked out everywhere.'
'Because he is a scumbag… for real!'
'I give you that… he is bad news!'
'But Brit… if this Jacques-Marie is somehow related to Fiona's family… then likely she is a distraction from the illegal income that her family is hiding from the authorities.'
'That may be the case… but why all the drama of making Fiona a suspect in a political double homicide?'
'That is correct… that goes a bit too far.'
'For what it is worth… Fiona is likely the victim in all of this.'
'My family always told me that the rich have many dark secrets.'
'They were telling you the truth!'
'This makes me question whether Fiona is the right woman for me…'
'She is the mother of your child… you have no choice!'

'I know… but...'
'No… buts!'
'Check this!'
'What is it?'
'It is a receipt…'
'I see…'
'3.000 Spanish Real to the President of a Filipino Company that operates in the Province of Costa Rica…'
'I never realised the Spanish Empire was so complicated.'
'Complicated, but stable!'
They heard footsteps.
'Run!'
The two ran out of the cabin and they arrived at the tunnel where they came in.
'You brought the receipt with you?'
'Oh… I forgot to put it back!'
'What do you want to do with it?'
'We can use it against Fiona's father.'
'Why would he pay 3.000 Spanish Real[14] to a Filipino Company?'
'Then we need to know what that Filipino Company is doing in Costa Rica.'
'Costa Rica is a few days away from here…'
'So is Guatemala City…'
'You want to go all the way to Cartago to find out what is going on?'
'You have a better idea?'
'We might get more help from the Foundation if we ask for it…'
'So, going back to the capital?'
'We are getting too involved in this!'
'I got you…'
'Look, it is enough that we are involved with Fiona… but we do not have to carry her baggage. We need to consider our own safety too!'
'I agree with you.'
'We already went too far by breaking into a military base. We can be imprisoned for years if the Royal Audiencia finds out.'
'They can only find out if one of us talk.'
'Watch out where you keep that receipt.'
'We will keep it with us till we arrive at the capital. I hope that the Foundation will help us as you suggested.'

[14] In today's money €19.125

'Then let us go!'
The two got on their horses and they headed towards the north.
Meanwhile, Fiona received a letter from her pen-pal Christina who lived in British-Honduras. Christina just got married to a British corn exporter. Fiona received several gifts with the letter, including some British sterling coins. While she counted the coins, the house cleaner informed her that a guy named 'Balduno' wanted to see her.
'Let him come in!'
'Yes, ma'am!'
Balduno arrived with a map under his arm.
'You got some news from the Foundation?'
'Well, I got some controversial stuff…'
'Sit down!'
Balduno sat down in one of the chairs and he placed the documents on the small table next to his chair.
'What is it?'
'Your uncle, Lionel Rodrigues, and Philemon Dominguez are in a feud concerning a debt that is owed to your family.'
'They are?'
'The money owed to your family was used to invest in this foundation and from what I found out; Philemon Dominguez is using this foundation to cover up their revenue from their Caribbean export.'
'I suspected something like that already…'
'It gets more interesting.'
'How?'
'Your father and your uncle have a half-brother… so, a half-uncle of yours… that lives in the Philippines.'
'What?'
'Hector Rodrigues was born to your grandfather and a Filipino slave. The man grew up working as a craftsman and he did one year of military service in New Spain. He eventually purchased the property where his maternal family was enslaved, and he turned it into a prosperous business. At age 29, he visited Quito to visit your father and that same year he met his other two brothers too…'
'This is the first time I hear about his existence…'
'He and your brothers agreed to use Costa Rica as a 'middle-ground' to transfer all their business. Costa Rica, having a low population, is a good place to locate goods before they are sold.'
'So, my half-uncle has a mine or some storage in Costa Rica?'

'He has five of them!'
'Five!'
'They are spread over the province… three of them are located just within a kilometre from a military base.'
'Hmmm…. is he working with the military?'
'I suspect he is…'
'So, what are they storing in Costa Rica?'
'Oil… expensive plant and fish oils that are produced in The Philippines.'
'Oil is an expensive business.'
'The amount of oil preserved there exceeds what is legally allowed. However, after four years… there is still no improvement.'
'Did he got fined?'
'Twice… and he paid all of it. Swiftly!'
'What do you mean with swiftly?'
'Due to his residence in Manila, he had a year to pay the 25.000 Spanish Real.[15] He paid it within just two months!'
'That is quick!'
'A bit too quick…'
'So… you think my father or one of my uncles, who are closer, paid for him?'
'That is the best explanation.'
'Good to know how much trust my father has in me…'
'Well, he might want to protect you.'
'Is this related to the killing of those politicians in Guadalajara?'
'No… this is something separate.'
'I think they have to be connected somehow…'
'Well, they might be…'
'What did you figure out?'
'The barrels of oil in Costa Rica got the attention of Nathaniel Alvaréz in 1794 and he purchased two properties in New Galicia to import Asian oil too… Well, in 1798… there was a big fire as the result of oil not being stored properly. Forty-eight workers died. The scandal was enormous, and this was what triggered an investigation from the Iberian Peninsula.'
'So, is that why those politicians came to inspect New Galicia?'
'Yes!'
'I have the feeling that Mister Alvaréz is involved with this.'

---

[15] In today's money €159.375

'Two pirates, *Clark Hansen* and *Herbert Johnson*, worked for Nathaniel between 1788 and 1796. The two men decided to remain in Quito after their 'retirement'. In March 1799, those two pirates were seen at the shores of New Galicia and several days later they were seen in Guadalajara. After the death of the two politicians… those two pirates were arrested. The British Minister, in Mexico City, pressured the Spanish court to let them go. This happened two months later. The men were commanded not to leave New Galicia until the investigation was completed.'
'So, they are still in New Galicia?'
'Yes.'
'Then the crime is solved.'
'It does not work that way… in politics.'
'Because it's the Alvaréz Cartel?'
'Well… it goes further than that… the incident in Guadalajara is rumoured to be orchestrated by the New Galician authorities in co-operation with Nathanael.'
'Now I understand why they want to blame it on my father!'
'They blamed it on you for a moment… to trick a response from your father and that worked!'
'Well, you cannot pick your parents…'
'I think it is best for you to remain in Guatemala… it is safer than living with your relatives.'
'I thought the same thing…'
'What will you do with Mathilde?'
'I will ask her to leave the moment my baby is born.'
'Kick her out as soon as possible! Her actions are unreasonable.'
'When was she ever reasonable? She never was! I have no idea what my uncle even saw in her.'
'What is your uncle like?'
'He is the kind of man that does not want to hear nonsense from anyone. He gets annoyed very quickly.'
'But he allows his wife to cross the Atlantic on her own to so-called visit her niece-in-law? Come on…'
'I know my uncle is filled with nonsense himself…'
'But…. There might be another reason why your aunt-in-law is around here.'
'What did you find out?'

‘Mathilde used to be acquainted with a choir that travelled through New Spain, giving performances… one of the sponsors of those events was an Oaxacan farmer named Calvin de Aragon y Playas. Calvin de Aragon is likely to have spent some time with the choir, including Mathilde. This was before she married your uncle.’
‘That is interesting!’
‘Apart from that… Calvin passed away four years ago. His son Luis took over his estate and he is a donor to the Foundation.’
‘Is she aware of it?’
‘I am not sure… Luis informed me that he kept receiving love letters towards his father… even after he was buried. He never responded.’
‘So, she just wants to catch up with her former lover… who is deceased.’
‘Exactly!’
‘I knew she had an ulterior motive for coming over!’
‘These are three of the letters she sent… they are from 1788. Two years after Calvin passed away.’
‘Well, she has quite a determined attitude!’
‘She likely married your uncle for his money and his influential position in Spain. Deceased Calvin cannot match your uncle.’
‘How much did Luis donate to us?’
‘Since his father passed away… 400 Spanish Real[16] a month. By now… around 16.000 Spanish Real.[17]’
‘He is a loyal donor.’
‘His father… in total, donated 30.000 Spanish Dollars[18] during his lifetime.’
‘What was Calvin’s interest in the Foundation?’
‘He has a Mayan grandfather, from his mother’s side, who supported him a lot during his youth. His father passed away at a young age during an accident in a mine. His mother dropped him at her parents, while she went out to earn some money. Calvin joined the Santiago Knights, in Guatemala City, when he was twenty… and it was there that he earned some good money. He used the money to reorganise an abandoned plot of land nearby – which the government assigned to him. This is how he became this prosperous farmer.’
‘Good success story.’

[16] In today’s money €2.550
[17] In today’s money €102.000
[18] In today’s money €191.250

'Well, there is a twist to it. Several of his relatives, from his father's side, suddenly died within a year after he received that plot of land. After they passed away, he earned more than all the other farmers in the Province of Oaxaca.'
'So, he became one of New Spain's wealthiest farmers… overnight?'
'That is what it is.'
'Do you know what the estate of Calvin is worth now?'
'Calvin had five sons; Luis is the oldest. Each son received 35.000 Spanish Dollars[19] and Luis received the whole estate which is worth around 140.000 Spanish Dollars.[20]'
'That is a LOT!'
'His sons are all living in Oaxaca and they purchased their own plots of land near the border with Guatemala.'
'Is land in the Kingdom of Mexico not expensive?'
'It is…'
'So, why did they not come over to Guatemala where land is cheaper, and the population is lower?'
'Oaxaca is well-maintained by the Spanish Crown, more than the provinces that make up Guatemala. So, that might be the reason.'
'Are their properties close to the shores?'
'Not really…'
'Those men do not add up.'
'I think they want to stay as far away from their deceased father's estate as soon as possible!'
'He must have been a horrible man.'
'Or… an accursed one.'
'Accursed by what?'
'Come on, Fiona…'
'Why would he be accursed?'
'Several relatives of him pass away within a year after he gets that abandoned plot of land… and after they all pass away his land becomes one of the best crop-producing lands in New Spain? He made a deal with the devil.'
'Then it was a crappy deal because he passed away early.'
'Whatever deal it was, it worked into bringing him wealth… but the side effects were horrible!'
'Then… why is Mathilde interested in a guy like that?'

[19] In today's money €223.125
[20] In today's money €892.500

‘She was a young lady, with almost no life experience… and she does not look at the bigger picture.’
‘Well, it is a good thing she married my uncle and not that dude.’
‘The dude was known to have many mistresses… and each of them died of horrible diseases within less than two years after he ended the affairs.’
‘Oh my God!’
‘That is the type of man he was…’
‘There are some creepy people living in New Spain…’
‘Everywhere, Fiona. This is a worldwide issue… creepy people pretending to be descent.’
‘Did you find out anything about Josephine?’
‘Hmm… I am still working on that.’
‘Good… I have the feeling she is up to something bad.’
‘If she is… we will sabotage her efforts.’
‘Good! I need to get a nap now… after dinner, you can return to the capital.’

10

That evening, Mathilde left quickly after completing dinner. She went to a French bakery to purchase some French tarts. After purchasing the French tarts, she left for the house. However, she never arrived. Two days later, Fiona became worried about her aunt-in-law.
She received a letter, from Rensy, that he was in Guatemala City doing some research together with Brittany. Balduno decided to stay with Fiona to find out what happened to her aunt-in-law. Balduno informed the local authorities about the missing. The guards, however, told him that there was not much they could do about the case. People went missing often in Nicaragua [more than in any other Spanish Province of New Spain].
That evening, Balduno found something interesting in Mathilde's room.
'Fiona, come and check this out!'
'What did you find?'
'Look at this!'
'Its', she checked the item out, 'a tiny box for tiny cigars.'
'Look at the mark on it…'
'That is produced somewhere in Chiapas.'
'Correct!'
'Products made in Chiapas are seldom sold in the rest of Guatemala… it is mainly people from the rest of the Spanish Main, in North America, that purchase them.'
'Furthermore, she just arrived from Spain and she did not visit any other place in the Spanish Main than Guatemala.'
'That means that…'
'She had some visit here.'
'Let me check it again.'
Fiona checked the box and then she found initials carved in it: L. de A.
'Luis de Aragon?'
'Likely!'
'So… the son of her former lover came looking for her?'
'Why would he do that? How does he know where I am?'
'Fiona… some people are flat out crazy!'
'So… Luis is likely involved in the kidnapping of my aunt-in-law?'
'We have no concrete evidence that she has been kidnapped.'
'What else could it be, Balduno? She does not just leave like that.'
'Fiona, you barely know this woman…'

‘Look, she is missing…’
‘That is none of your concern now. Let me go after it. You need to focus on you and Rensy.’
‘He is in the capital now.’
‘Doing what?’
‘He is with Brittany.’
‘Oh…’
‘No… he is not cheating. He is on some investigation that relates to my father somehow. There is some military involvement.’
‘What does he know?’
‘He will give me the receipt when he comes back to Masaya.’
‘I will be waiting for those receipts too.’
‘Maybe it is better for me not to remain over here.’
‘Where do you plan to go then?’
‘What if I move further to Bocas del Toro?’
‘You want to go all the way to the border of Guatemala?’
‘It might be safer for me there… away from all of this.’
‘Hmm…. Do you have an address?’
‘I will find some guesthouse to stay at.’
‘I will bring you and then I will return to the capital. Meanwhile, we need to leave some note for Rensy in case he arrives.’
‘Good!’
Right when Balduno was writing the note, he felt the need to pick up the box again. When he checked the box, he found a folded piece of paper hidden in it.
‘Fiona… check this!’
‘Where did you get this from?’
‘It was hidden in the box.’
‘What does it say?’

The safe is in the San Francisco Tavern in Cartago. Second floor, third room next to the stairs. Behind the Mary painting, you will find the key. The safe is in the corner, at the window.

‘A safe?’
‘If this is from Luis… he is hiding something there.’
‘Hmm… it might be close to one of the oil reserves of my half-uncle.’
‘I am not sure that connection can be made.’
‘There is only one way to find out.’
‘So, you want to go over there?’

'You go there and let me know what you find out. I will stay here… it is better for Rensy to find me here than for me to suddenly relocate without his knowledge.'
'I think that is better indeed.'
'Let me know what you find out!'
'If anything, weird goes down… get the first chariot to the Foundation.'
'I will!'
Balduno arrived two days later in Cartago where he visited the San Francisco Tavern. He paid the fee for two nights. His room was next to the alleged room where a safe was hidden. During the evening, the guesthouse was almost empty. He took his opportunity to break into the room and to figure it out. The room was beautifully decorated, and he found the Mary painting on the wall. The key was there also. He checked every corner. He did not find a safe. He then pulled the carpet up and he found one of the corners to have broken planks. He pulled up the planks and he found a small safe. It took him a while, but he got the safe out of the ground.
At that point, he heard people coming into the guesthouse. He moved quickly to his own room with the safe. After taking a little nap, he opened the safe.
The safe contained a gun, a pack of ammunition, a small drawn portrait of a young lady and 30 Spanish Escudo coins.[21] After checking the picture, he realised that the drawn woman looked quite like Fiona.
The same night, he rode back to Masaya and he found Fiona doing the dishes when he arrived at the house.
'Fiona!'
'Wow… that is quick… you only took four days?'
'Look!', he placed the box on the table, and he opened it. 'check it out!'
'Oh… God!'
'This image here… is an image of you! Look in the mirror and check this image… it is quite similar.'
'That gun seems new!'
'It is a new gun! This model has been adopted in Spain just two years ago. It is widely used in Austria.'
'So… someone has placed a hit on my life?'
'That is what the evidence shows.'
'Who could it be?'
'That is not relevant now…'

[21] In today's money €3.060

'But… what about the box for tiny cigars? Who left it? I mean… my aunt-in-law is missing, we found this weird box in her room, in the box was a note… we followed the note and now we found out that someone hired a hitman. And we think that the initials refer to Luis de Aragon.'
'Hmm….'
'This is a bit overwhelming for me…'
'Do not blame yourself.'
'Hold on…'
'What is wrong?'
'You mentioned that Luis de Aragon donated quite some money to the Foundation. The first day I took office, I remember that one donor wanted to purchase the Foundation from its Galician owners. I told the departing secretary to write a letter to the donor that it was out of question. It was a man living in Oaxaca.'
'Hmm… so, Luis wants to purchase the Foundation. With what money?'
'He offered 350.000 Spanish Real[22] for it.'
'What?!'
'I know… I was surprised myself.'
'Where does he get all that money from?'
'How should I know? I did not even care to investigate which donor it was.'
'Why did you not?'
'I was just President for several hours and I did not want to spoil the moment.'
'You do realise that the offer was a red flag, right?'
'I do now… back then I did not even register it as something odd… only that the price was so high.'
'So, this Luis might want to get rid of you to get the Foundation.'
'Even if that is the case, the Foundation is owned by the Ramos and Dominguez families. He should write a petition to Spain to purchase it from them!'
'So, let me picture this… the Dominguez Household, one of the owners of this Foundation, owes your family money. The wife of the family leader, your uncle, is the former lover of the father of the man… who wants to purchase the Foundation.'
'There is no such thing as coincidence…'

[22] In today's money €2.231.250

‘That means that YOU are considered a hindrance to someone’s agenda.’
‘My dad’s agenda likely… he always wanted more money to go to South America instead of Spain… you know that.’
‘So, you think that the oil reserves in Costa Rica are meant to generate revenue for projects in South America?’
‘Likely it is… but… I do not think my dad is behind this assassination plot. He loves me.’
‘Well… I do not think it is your dad that is behind this. Either that half-uncle of yours… or Luis.’
‘Luis might want to Foundation. What does my half-uncle want? He lives all the way in The Philippines!’
‘Maybe some tragic distraction from the whole operation.’
‘How are we even sure my half-uncle is in The Philippines? He might be around here, and nobody knows about it. From what I understand about him, he is a dark figure. Dark figures tend to be somehow hidden from the community.’
‘Correct! I do not have resources however to figure out if he is actually in Asia.’
‘Not needed… We will just wait for Rensy to contact us.’
‘He still did not contact you?’
‘He did not.’
‘Did he run away with that British woman?’
‘No… Brittany and Josephine are quite close. So, Brittany would never do that.’
‘Speaking about Josephine… I found out something odd about her.’
‘What is that?’
‘This woman has not been in contact with her relatives at all.’
‘Hmm…. What is odd about that?’
‘She is a female… and females crave community peace. She has not exchanged a single letter with her relatives in Britain since moving here. She has also not been seen with any man recently.’
‘Odd…’
‘Furthermore, she likes to paint her hair often… something that others consider witchy.’
‘Maybe she is a witch indeed.’
‘That being the case, she risks an execution by the public.’

‘Now that you mention it… one time she had blonde hair… then she had orange hair… then she had red hair… then she made it greyish… she is always changing it.’
‘Why?’
‘She is not happy with how God made her.’
‘That means she is reprobate… right?’
‘Hmm… maybe not reprobate… but she is anxious about something!’
‘In any case… she is not working. She also has no man providing for her. So… how does she take care of herself?’
‘Maybe she is selling her ass.’
‘Well… she is quite anti-social from time to time.’
‘Whatever she does, as long as she does not cause any unnecessary harm… I am fine with it.’
‘So, do you think she stole the money from the treasury?’
‘Maybe she did…’
At that moment, Huyên walked in with some groceries.
‘Does she understand us?’
‘Her Spanish is quite weak…’
‘She should learn it as soon as possible… if she plans to live in Spanish America. It is not called **Spanish** America for nothing!’
‘That is right!’
‘Anyway, I need to go now… let me know if Rensy comes by.’
‘Good!’
After Balduno left, Huyên poked Fiona’s arm.
‘We… need… talk now.’
‘Ah… your Spanish is getting better.’
‘Thanks. But… we need talk…’
‘What is it about?’
‘Mathilde is dead.’
‘Dead?’
‘Killed. You were… eating.’
‘Where was the last time you saw her?’
‘Morning. Walked outside. Tiny man… stabbing.’
‘She was stabbed. You saw it happen?’
‘Yes!’
‘Why did you not tell me?’
‘I afraid…’
‘Do not talk about this with anyone… did the man have this box with him?’

‘Box’, Huyên touched the box, ‘gift for Rensy from killer.’
‘What?’
‘Killer wanted talk to Rensy…’
‘Oh… Ok. I get it!’
Fiona went to the bedroom where she took a nap. She was exhausted by the new revelations of the case. When she woke up three hours later, she heard Huyên cooking. She was not hungry, but she appreciated Huyên’s effort.
The next day in Guatemala City, Brittany, Josephine and Balduno broke into the building that was often used by the Royal Chamber of Commerce. The institution used several buildings to remain unpredictable.
‘What are we exactly looking for her?’
‘Just keep on digging.’
‘Where?’
‘In this basement… it should be here somewhere.’
‘At least give me a sign.’
‘You find any human remains…’
‘Oh dear…’
‘Keep on digging…’
‘Hold on…’
The other two ran to where Josephine was digging.
‘It is a hand…’
‘It looks a bit fresh.’
‘It is smelling also.’
‘Oh God!’
‘What do we do now?’
‘We have to tell somebody!’
‘Telling them that we broke into a government building and began looking for corpses?’
‘Finish digging first!’
The three dug up the body and it was a young man. A criollo or peninsulares, based on his looks.
‘How will be justify this?’
‘Hold on… check his purse.’
‘When they checked his purse, they found a compass, 10 Spanish escudo coins, worth 160 Spanish Real and two bullets… unused.’
‘Suicide?’
‘I see no gun nor a gunshot to any part of the body.’

‘Is Rensy still on the outlook?’
‘He is!’
‘Who was this man?’
‘Look!’
Josephine got a tiny notebook from his pocket.

It has been five hours since I arrived in Acapulco. The next ship will depart tomorrow. I will arrive somewhere in the Province of Chiapas, close to Guatemala City.

‘That means he came from Asia, right?’
‘Likely from The Philippines.’
‘Look at this!’
‘Oh gross…’, Brittany pointed towards the belly, ‘he was stabbed to death, at least twenty times.’
‘That is something personal!’
‘Hold on… I got a name… Hector.’
‘Hector? Oh God no…’
‘What is it, Balduno?’
‘This is Fiona’s uncle. Half-uncle. He has a Filipino mother.’
‘That explained the skin that is a bit tannish.’
‘Wait… so, Fiona’s uncle is killed and buried here?!’
‘That is what is appears too…’
‘Hmm… we need to warn someone about this. I will take care of this. Let us get out of here before we are caught!’
When they came outside, Rensy noticed their destressed looks.
‘What is going on?’
‘Rensy… it is Fiona’s half-uncle. We found him. Buried.’
‘Oh God!’
‘I know…’
‘So, someone is after Fiona’s life… her half-aunt went missing and her half-uncle has been assassinated. Does it get any worse?’
‘Not if we stop this.’
‘How? I have no experience in solving crime! Half of my relatives are involved in crime!’
‘We need to get back into the Foundation!’
‘Huyên and Fiona are safe there, right?’
‘Yes…I informed some of the local guards and they are checking the house.’
‘Come!’

The next morning, the authorities emptied the building that was rented by the Royal Chamber of Commerce. The building became a forbidden property for people to enter. The priests came and they prepared the body for a funeral. Due to the absence of direct relatives, Fiona was picked up to attend the funeral (which she reluctantly did). After the funeral, the body was laid to rest in a cemetery near the old capital of Guatemala. The local authorities registered *Hector Henrique Rodrigues y May* as deceased.
Fiona remained at the capital, assisted by Huyên. The notarial officer of the capital approach Fiona concerning the inheritance of her half-uncle.
'Miss Rodrigues, I know this is a difficult time for you… but this is something we need to go through.'
'Look, I have a very rough time behind me, and I just buried an uncle I never knew I had!'
'Hector left you something.'
'What did he leave to me?'
'There are two tiny farms located in the south of Guatemala.'
'Where exactly?'
'In Costa Rica.'
'Ah', Fiona remembered that those two farms were where her uncles and father kept their oil reserve, 'that is interesting.'
'The rest of his properties, in The Philippines, will go to his son, Marco. There is a report that has been mail yesterday to Manila. Within a month, Marco will hear the horrible news about his father.'
'How old was my uncle?'
'He was fifty-two. His son Marco is twenty-seven.'
'Will you inform his other siblings?'
'I will… next week. Right now, this needs to be settled first. The body will remain in the graveyard near Antigua Guatemala… unless the family decides that the body needs to be relocated. In that case, the judge will have the final say.'
'Understood!'
'Just sign here… and the two plots of land in the south are yours… including all the content found on the properties. I think I do not have to explain to you what those are.'
'I know…'
'Sign here!'
Fiona singed and afterwards she received a receipt of her reception.

'The authorities in Costa Rica need to be informed. Wait two weeks before taking any action, please.'
'I will wait!'
'That is, it!'
'Sir, one more thing…'
'What?'
'Can did remain between us?'
'That is up to you!'
'Good, have a nice day!'
When she arrived at the Foundation, she kept herself to herself. She even told Huyên to leave her alone for a moment.
The next day, she visited church where she wept. She realised after signing the inheritance agreement that she just lost a relative that will never come back. He was gone. FOR GOOD!

11

For the remainder of her pregnancy, things remained quiet around her. This was something she appreciated. The day she gave birth, Rensy was present – as well as her other staff-members.

'It is a baby girl!'

Rensy was filled with gladness. He was a father of a daughter. The Foundation even held a small party to celebrate the birth of their daughter. Nine days after the birth of their daughter, however, Rensy disappeared without saying anything. The mail delivered told Fiona that he moved back to his hometown in the south. He left after registering his daughter at the public registry. The couple decided to call their daughter Gabrielle.

The day after Rensy suddenly left, Fiona accepted the fact that he likely declined his duty of fatherhood. The baby was now only ten days old. The same day, the baby was baptised in the church in the capital.

After the baptism of Gabrielle, Balduno handed Fiona a note from a Spanish-speaking Garifuna chief, Mauro, that established his own small confederacy in the West of the Province of Honduras.

'Who is this Mauro?'

'He is the leader of a tiny tribe of Garinagu people… His confederacy consisted out of eight extended households, together 1.543 people and 122 native mercenaries as his private army.'

'That is impressive!'

'His confederacy was officially established in 1791. But… it is not recognised by the Spanish government yet.'

'Not yet?'

'Chief Mauro paid a voluntary tribute to the Royal Audiencia of Guatemala, last month, which bribed the Spanish officials to look the other way…'

'How much did he pay?'

'2.500 Spanish Dollars.[23]'

'He is serious about this…'

'The confederacy eventually constructed four villages near Copán as their territory. When the villages were completed, in 1793, the confederate people requested their leader to secure support for them

[23] In today's money €127.500

from the urban population in Guatemala City. That has not worked out well till this day.'
'That has been seven years.'
'So… he requests help from our foundation.'
'Our foundation is aimed for Mayan people…'
'He wants to trade with the Mayans… but he wants to make a good impression.'
'So… for the past seven years he has been the leader of a tiny tribe… and he failed in securing trade?'
'He trades with Negroes from St. Vincent and from the East of Spanish Honduras. However, his people need more income and Mayan textile is quite popular worldwide.'
'We are not a business broker.'
'No… but we are well respected by the Mayan community.'
'He invites us', she read the letter, 'to the wedding of his son, Jio.'
'When does it take place?'
'Five days from now…'
'What do you think?'
'Well, after the whole situation with Rensy… I am in a party mood.'
'Where is he?'
'He left without telling me anything… he is likely back in Matagalpa.'
'I never really considered him a good guy to begin with.'
'Well, it is a bit too late for that now… I already give birth to our baby and he will have to be part of my life whether I like it or not.'
'I do not think he wants to be part of your life, or else he would be here.'
'True to that…'
'In any case… you do have the baby to look after.'
'Maybe we should just decline… and invite him to the capital.'
'If you think that is better… we will.'
'Just check where Rensy is for me.'
'I will… after arranging this with the Garifuna chief.'
That night, she went to a public spa to get some relief from all that just happened past days. She was not even shocked that Rensy just 'took off'. She noticed symptoms for a while that Rensy was not willing to be part of her toxic family. She already made peace with it before their daughter was born. While being at the bathhouse, Huyên came to her.
'Mistress…'
'What is wrong, Huyên?'

'You need to come!'
'What?'
'Come!'
'Wait!'
She got out of the pond and she dried herself with the towel.
'Give me a minute!'
Ten minutes later, she was wearing her heels, make-up, as well as her blue dress. She walked outside with Huyên.
'Your aunt, Mathilde. Has been found.'
'Good… where is she?'
'She is dead.'
'Oh dear?'
'A body was found near the Lake of Masaya. Some children were playing around when one of the street dogs began to dig in the ground and encountered a human hand.'
'How was she identified.'
'She had a necklace as well as a tiny portrait of her and her husband, painted in Spain, in her wallet.'
'How long has she been dead?'
'The detectives assume at least four months...'
'Where is the body now?'
'The body has been placed in a local church, in Costa Rica. The body will be transported to Spain four days from now.'
'Is my uncle informed?'
'The body was discovered a week ago. He will be informed when the body arrives in Cadiz.'
'This is a dark season for my relatives.'
'Did you inform your father about Gabrielle?'
'I did… the letter should have arrived by now. He will be glad!'
'That is nice!'
'Your Spanish has improved significantly!'
'Thanks!'
'How is your father?'
'He is greedy for money, as always!'
'Recognisable!'
'What will you do about Rensy?'
'I will let that work out on its own. My focus on now on my little baby girl and I am meeting a chieftain soon.'
'Chieftain?'

‘A Black chieftain that governs a small community in the West of Honduras.’
‘Is it a rival to Spanish rule?’
‘No… Honduras has many black confederacies that are not recognised by the Spanish government. However, they are tolerated because they help maintaining stability in this kingdom.’
‘Can I be there?’
‘Of course! Just do not say anything.’
‘Sure!’
‘Come… I need some spicy dish now.’
‘All right!’
Balduno received a response from the Garifuna court and the chieftain responded favourably towards a meeting with Balduno and the President (which is, Fiona). Fiona’s Presidency was extended by being re-elected. The meeting was to happen next week Wednesday at the Foundation’s garden. It was now Sunday night when the confirmation arrived by mail. Balduno rushed to Fiona’s office, where she was listening to some flute music played by Huyên.
‘Fiona, he is arriving next week Wednesday around 11:00 in the morning.’
‘That is good news! Is he coming alone?’
‘He will arrive with his First Minister, ten of his private guards, and two of his wives.’
‘Two of his wives?’
‘He has five wives and eighteen children.’
‘Wow!’
‘His two wives are from Barbados… and they speak English well.’
‘Good! Then make sure everything is prepared for when they come. I will let Huyên babysit Gabrielle for the time he is here.’
‘Who do you want to be there?’
‘You will be there… I will be of course. You know, I want Huyên to be there. I will hire a nanny for Gabrielle. Do we have an interpreter?’
‘He speaks English… so, one of his wives may be the interpreter.’
‘Hmm…. That is fine then.’
‘What do we prepre?’
‘Prepare some feast… good, fresh meat, some good salads, and some French wines. It will be great.’
‘Got it!’
After he left, Huyên took a pause.

'Why did you stop?'
'You really want me to be there?'
'Why not?'
'I am just your servant?'
'You are one of my closest friends now. So, I want you to be there. Besides, you are a good musician. You can entertain our visitors.'
'I surely will!'
'By the way, my father told me that Luis de Aragon was likely the one behind Mathilde's murder.'
'How does your father know?'
'Luis was never in agreement with his father's infatuation with her…'
'Hmmm… but his father was already dead. Why would he go after Mathilde?'
'Mathilde informed Luis that she was coming, but Mathilde thought that it was his father who would read the letters. It appears that Mathilde had a miscarriage. However, rumours were that she had an abortion because she later met your uncle when she arrived in Spain.'
'Oh gosh…'
'So… Luis likely avenged his unborn sibling…'
'Is it possible that this is what led to the heartache and early dead of Calvin?'
'That might be so…'
'In any case, Luis is not charged because there is no evidence besides me seeing a short guy. I am not even sure if that short guy was Luis, and I never met Luis.'
'It is best to keep your mouth shut. Let it rest. Mathilde will be buried in Spain once her body arrives and live will go on.'
'That is the reason why I always keep myself a bit... secluded from the rest. I do not want to be caught up in the conflicts of others. Conflicts tend to escalate quickly.'
'I understand that.'
'About this Mauro I…'
'What does he really want from us?'
'He comes for trade.'
'There are trade fraternities here in Guatemala City as well as in the provincial capitals of Guatemala. Why is he not going there?'
'He speaks no Spanish…'
'He has five wives and an excessively big household. One of his wives, of at least some of his in-laws, can easily interpret for him.

Furthermore, he established his community in Spanish America, so he should learn Spanish as soon as possible!'
'I agree...'
'I think he knows something about this foundation.'
'This foundation is filled with weird secrets... maybe he knows more than I do!'
'What will you do after your term is over?'
'Well, due to my pregnancy I was re-elected. Hmm... I do not know. My term will end within four months I think.'
'What will you do?'
'I might move to Costa Rica... with Gabrielle. Or... maybe I can join Rensy somewhere in Nicaragua. I will see!'
'Think wisely... your decisions will affect Gabrielle too!'
'I know... I know!'
While they still spoke, someone knocked on the door.
'Come in!'
'Fiona', it was Rensy, 'we need to talk!'
'Huyên... leave us!'
Huyên left swiftly and she closed the door behind her.
'Fiona...'
'What were you thinking!', she slapped him in the face, 'Leaving me behind with our daughter like that?'
'Look...'
'Where were you?!'
'I was thinking.'
'Thinking about what?'
'I cannot do this...'
'What not?'
'Living with you...'
'Is it because of the baby?'
'No... I love our daughter... I do. However, you and your family. It is too much for me. I am not able to live like that... always looking behind me to see if there is danger or not.'
'I am glad you are honest about it.'
'I want to be able to see our daughter.'
'You will be able to see her... if you pay child support. 150 Real per month.'
'That is a lot!'
'Well, that is to make sure you remain a father figure in her life.'

'Come on…'
'Ey! You are the one who suddenly left both of us… without any explanation. What kind of man does that?'
'That is a flaw of mine… I am working on it.'
'I am sure you do… is there anyone else?'
'Fiona…'
'Is there someone else?'
'She is a woman from a rival neighbourhood. We have been seeing each other for two months now.'
'Look, there is no use for use to argue and to fight a war. You do not want to be with me… I am not going to force you. That will not benefit anyone, especially not our daughter. However, you will pay the child support!'
'I will…'
'You will only visit her on appointment!'
'Got it!'
'And Rensy…'
'What?'
'GET OUT!'
Rensy left.
Huyên came back in.
'That was rough of you!'
'Well, I had to be… he is a coward and he now wants to pretend as if nothing happened. I do not fall for that.'
'Are you even sure it is safe to let Gabrielle with him alone?'
'That will not happen. He will only have supervised visits with our daughter. As simple as that.'
'You managed that well…'
'I could not pretend like nothing ever happened. The betrayal still hurts, so I was not really happy to see him.'
'Nobody can blame you.'
'He just left his 10-day-old daughter for some whore that he just met two months ago.'
'Her relatives might not be as challenging as yours.'
'He wanted to have sex with me… but he was not willing know who he was having sex with?'
'He is a man… he thinks differently.'
'Ah well… I hope I do not see him here any time soon. I am focussing now on the future.'

‘He will be part of that.’
‘A small part, I hope!’
‘Shall I continue with the song?’
‘Yes, please!’
The next morning, Balduno received a letter from Philemon Dominguez who instructed that the ‘Santa Barbara Foundation for the Alleviation of The Mayans of The Kingdom of Guatemala’ should refrain from getting into bargains with native confederacies and ‘black communities’ that reside in Guatemala. Balduno, however, pretended as if he did not read the instruction and he put the letter away. He was not willing to cancel the meeting with Mauro.
A week later, Mauro and his crew arrived in Guatemala City where they resided in a Mayan-owned Inn. Balduno secretly met with the ‘First Minister’ of Mauro, who was really his Spanish speaking half-brother who arranged Mauro’s financial affairs. The half-brother used the Spanish name Maduro. The two met at a Mayan fountain nearby.
‘Maduro!’
‘Is everything arranged?’
‘Yes!’, he received the bag with money from Maduro, ‘your brother will meet the duchess the day after tomorrow.’
‘That is 200 Spanish Escudos and 350 Spanish Dollars.’
‘That is 6.000 Spanish Real worth of coins… as we agreed.’
‘Whatever you want to use it for… do it wisely. You do not earn that much as staff member of a foundation.’
‘I know what I am doing… just make sure you bring your brother on time.’
‘We are quite punctual!’
‘Good!’
That evening, Balduno met with several of his creditors, and he paid off the 1.200 Spanish Real of debt he owed the four men. He even paid each 10 Spanish Real of interest. The men were surprised with the sudden one-time payment. The creditors expected him to pay them back within a year. The creditors even became suspicious of how he got the money so quickly – after less than four months.
‘Are you trapping us, Balduno?’
‘What are you talking about?’
‘You got your money as well as interest! The interest was not even agreed, that is my thank you for helping me out.’
‘Did you go to another money lender to pay us back?’

‘No… I got some revenue from some other enterprise of mine and I withdrew the revenue from it.’
The creditors looked at each other and none of them believed what he said.
‘In any case, we will never loan you any cash again. Not because we do not trust you to pa us back… but… you are bad news… man.’
One of the creditors smacked him in the belly, before they left.
‘People like us are not the type of folks you should want to be involved with. Let that be a lesson. Avoid folks like us! Got it!’
‘Got it…’
The men left. The next day, he recovered from the slap in his belly. Wednesday morning, he was briefly followed when he walked back from the public washing pond where he just washed his clothes earlier. He placed his clothes in front of the fireplace to make them dry. Later that morning, he arrived at the Foundation where Fiona and Huyên were already awaiting him.
‘Whoa… why dressed so fancy?’
‘Well, being well dressed is a form of good manners.’
‘I agree…’
‘Furthermore, it is a political leader that we are meeting. I treat him with the same honour as if he were a governor or a foreign diplomat.’
‘So, you recognise the Black confederacies?’
‘Yeah… they deserve their recognition. Without their ancestors, the Spanish Empire would not even exist to begin with!’
‘Correct!’
Huyên wore a long-pink dress with a thick necklace. Fiona wore a shorter dress, black, with an opening at her left thigh that ended all the way where her waste began. She has a silver waist belt that kept the dress together. She wore black sandals with small heels attached to them. She also wore bright red lipstick to be more appealing.
‘Is that dress not a bit too revealing, Fiona?’
‘Well, it is like a Greek party dress… so, it is permissible.’
‘If you say so…’
The desk where Fiona sat was removed. Instead, there were two chairs, a small round table in front of them, and a couch for the rest of the people that would arrive. Huyên held an instrument. She was ready to play it.
‘So, we are all ready?’
‘We are…’

'I will check if Mauro is already here!'
'Good!'
After a half hour, a staff member came in to warn them that their visitors were arriving.
'You are ready? Huyên?'
'Ready, ma'am!'
The door opened. Balduno walked in. Behind him, there was a relatively short black male dressed in a sailor's outfit. Behind the man with a sailor's outfit, there were two fair dark-skinned women, decorated in colourful African clothes. Behind the two women was a man dressed in something that seems like a priest's garment with a hoody.
'Thank you all for being here! I am Balduno Casighari, Vice-President of the Santa Barbara Foundation. This here is Huyên Nyu, one of our Asian musicians, and this is Fiona Rodrigues, Duchess of Amatique, our current President.'
'Nice to meet you all!', stood up from her chair and she greeted each of them, 'Thank you for being here!'
Huyên followed her example.
'Miss Rodrigues, this is Maduro, the First Minister of the Maurice Confederacy.'
'Nice to meet you, Miss Rodrigues!'
'Miss Rodrigues, these are the two wives of His Excellency, Mauro I, Kandate and Kethura.'
'Nice to meet you ladies!'
'Miss Rodrigues, this is His Excellency, Mauro I, chieftain of the Maurice Confederacy.'
'Welcome to the Santa Barbara Foundation, Your Excellency!'
She embraced him and she sat back into her chair.
When everyone was seated, wine was served while Huyên played a beautiful Asian song. Maduro and Balduno kept the conversation going. Mauro, however, was not saying anything at all. After a half-hour, the company went to the garden where there was a banquet.
During the bankquet, Kandate pulled Fiona aside.
'Ma'am… can we talk?'
'Yeah… sure!'
'As you know, His Excellency does not master Spanish that well. He can understand some stuff. He is fluent in English.'
'Oh… I do not speak English, ma'am.'

'That is why me, and my sister-wife, are here to help our husband out.'
'So... what is it?'
'Well, Mauro does want to trade... he has enough to purchase much merchandise from the Mayans on the spot.'
'On the spot?'
'Your foundation looks after impoverish Mayan towns, right?'
'Yes, most of them are located between the capital and the Pacific Ocean...'
'Well, Mauro is willing to import much chocolate, Mayan beer as well as textile for his people.'
'That is good news!'
'Well, our First Minister found out that you owned barrels of Asian oil.'
'Wow... how did he found out?'
'This is a small world. Asian oil is quite expensive... but the storage of it is also forbidden in big quantities.'
'Correct. I still did not find a way to sell those 400 sealed barrels of oil.'
Kandate knew very well that the Foundation was used to coverup income from Spanish families in Spain. She also knew very well that much of the donated money never goes to any of the 'disadvantaged Mayans' that live near the Pacific. She realised that Fiona was naïve for believing that the Foundation did help impoverished Mayans.
'Look... you have an oil issue to deal with... as well as the legitimacy of this Foundation and our confederacy needs a new queen consort.'
'Queen consort?'
'Mauro longs for a new beauty at his court.'
'Yeah... but he already has both of you and three others... hahah.'
'Well, for the acceptance of our community... it is best for Mauro to have Spanish duchess as a consort. Think about it, it will be a good succession after your term as President ends here.'
'Hmm.... Why does Mauro not say anything?'
'He is not a talker... he is a doer. There is a chariot, outside of this building, waiting for you. Just step in... and get acquainted with him. I see you already dressed up for the occasion.'
'The chariot is already here?'
'Yeah...'
Fiona looked around and he indeed did not see Mauro anywhere. The donation will be handed over to Balduno after your one-on-one meeting with the chief has taken place.

She walked towards the chariot, when she opened the door, she did not see anyone inside of it. She sat down and she waited. Just several seconds later, Mauro stepped in.
'Oh Hi…'
Mauro held Fiona's hand as the chariot rode away. She smiled and she looked outside of the chariot's window.
Later that afternoon, Balduno and Maduro signed a contract that transferred 50.000 Spanish Real[24] into the account of the Foundation. The money was stored at a notary office in Guatemala City. That night, the chariot passed by the Copán district which was at the border of the Province of Honduras and the Chiquimula District. After crossing the border, the chariot turned towards the north and it stopped a half-hour later at a small village. The village contained a big house.
'Is this your place?'
Everyone got out. The people around did not pay much attention to them. At that moment, someone opened the door for them, and they were led in. The house was decorated in a modern-French style. There was a tale in the centre of a room that they entered. At the window there was this soft twin bed, a nightstand, and a small book shelve. At the table there was a chair, with some flowers, a feather, and a pot of ink. She sat down, while Mauro left the room. She read the document that was in front of her. It was in English and Spanish. The contract promised that she would become a part of Mauro's household and that she would become entitled to accessing all his properties as well as managing a portion of his local trade. The Foundation would get a one-time donation of 50.000 Spanish Real on behalf of the public that the organisation aimed to help. In exchange, her barrels of oil would become the property of Mauro's confederacy and this implied that Fiona was relieved from paying taxes over the properties as well as the fines for (illegally) stored goods. Furthermore, she would, as one of his consorts, look after his other children and the community affairs.
Ten minutes later, she opened the door and invited Mauro in.
'Here!'
The document was signed. On every page. She added one condition to the written agreement.
'You will have to learn Spanish, at some point!'
She held his hand, they kissed, and he closed the door behind them. She turned off the candles as well as closing the curtains.

---

[24] In today's money €318.750

12

The next morning, Fiona woke up to find that Mauro was already awake. She looked outside of the window and she saw him talking to some of the elderly visitors. After washing herself in the backyard, she asked one of the house staff [in Spanish] if she could get a ride back to the capital. At that same moment, Maduro walked in.
'Good morning, Miss Rodrigues.'
'Hey… Maduro. Where is your brother?'
'He is arranging some community stuff. He will be back soon. You guys spend some time together, I see.'
'You are here to get the contract?'
'I already got one of the copies you signed.'
'I just want one more thing: I want Huyên to join me here.'
'I will tell Mauro that…'
'My Presidential term will end within four months. So, the remainder of that time I would like to remain over here. Balduno as the vice-president can arrange things on my behalf.'
'Got it!'
'One thing…'
'…'
'How did you find out about the oil?'
'Before your uncle was killed, he wanted to sell the oil to Mauro. Mauro was read to pay… but then he suddenly was unreachable. It took a month before we heard about his death. Mauro was still into the oil… but at the same time… he also wanted a new adventure. So, when he found out that Hector's niece inherited Hector's possessions in Guatemala… he sent me to Guatemala City to check who you were. I reported to him how well-behaved and physically attractive you were. He wanted me to arrange a meeting to invite you as his new bride. Well, I did it a bit differently… I made sure both the Foundation as well as you would be far better off.'
'Understood.'
'Look, you will get along well with your fellow consorts as well as with your new man.'
'I am looking forward to it… I just hope he learns Spanish quickly.'
'Maybe YOU can teach him.'
'Hmm… I did not think about that yet.'
'It is a suggestion.'

'I will consider it. Just get Huyên here. Check if she wants to become a consort also… if not… she can become my close servant here too.'
'Just explore the place a little bit!'
'I will!'
A week afterwards, Christine, Huyên as well as all their belongings arrived in the village. The Foundation bought up much of the export and products of the estranged Mayan villages as agreed in the agreement. The sudden activities of the Foundation caught the attention of the rich and wealthy in the Province of San Salvador. On the request of Fiona, Mauro donated another 40.000 Spanish Real[25] into the foundation after just one month of her living in his household. The second financial boost triggered anger into the rich and wealthy of San Salvador who always prided themselves into being better off than the Mayan towns 'near the capital'.
At the same time, 300 vessels of oil, in total 1.500 litre, was sold to Dutch importers. The total revenue of the sale was 1.500.000 Spanish Real.[26] From this 80.000 Spanish Real[27] went to transportation and administrative costs and 100.000 Spanish Real[28] to taxes. The remainder 1.320.000 Spanish Real[29] was stored in the treasury of Mauro's Confederacy. Maduro made sure the Dutch importers paid the highest price for each decilitre of oil – which was four times the price it costed in Asia. The remainder 100 vessels of oil, in Costa Rica, remained hidden as a back-up.
The sale of most of the oil came right on time: an inspection by the provincial authorities had fined many people that held smuggled goods on their properties. Some of the property owners were even sentenced to prison sentences. Since Fiona conceded her inheritance, from her half-uncle to Mauro meant that she avoided prosecution. Furthermore, Mauro was a community leader and community leaders received some allowances by the Spanish government. Mauro's Household increased due to his investment in Fiona and the Foundation: from only 300.000 Spanish Real[30]… losing 90.000… His household now possessed 1.650.000 Spanish Real.[31] The sudden increase of Mauro's household

---

[25] In today's money €255.000
[26] In today's money €9.562.500
[27] In today's money €510.000
[28] In today's money €637.500
[29] In today's money €8.415.000
[30] In today's money €1.912.000
[31] In today's money €10.518.750

empowered him to invest in his people immediately. He granted subsidies for farming, breeding livestock as well as building better houses – all a total of 500.000 Spanish Real.[32]
It was now two months since Fiona became part of Mauro's household and by now the Santa Barbara Foundation gained many enemies in the city of San Salvador as well as in the District of Quetzaltenango. The 90.000 Spanish Real[33] that Mauro invested in the Mayan people caused a financial breakthrough for many Mayan households. The financial breakthrough of those Mayan households implied that they were less reliant as collateral for the rich that exploited them. There were riots in San Salvador against the 'prosperity of the pagans' that suddenly came out of nowhere. The anger in the public was so big that some even organised themselves as armed mobs to march towards the Mayan towns to 'teach those pagans a lesson'. The emergence of the bitterness in society alarmed the Royal Audiencia immediately. The reported incidents were many. The Royal Audiencia sent an additional 2.000 soldiers to the city of San Salvador to calm down the situation. An additional 1.500 soldiers and 800 volunteers were sent to the District of Quetzaltenango to shut down any mob operation.
Within a week, the troops were localised in the two places and the situation in Quetzaltenango calmed down quickly when the public noticed the abundance of troops that arrived. However, the dissatisfaction with the prosperity of the formerly disadvantaged Mayan towns did not disappear. In San Salvador there was a clash between the troops and rioters: 4 people died, 42 were wounded and 92 were arrested. After the clash between the public and the troops, the situation calmed down externally. However, the longing for 'payback' against their former scapegoats grew.
Brittany and Josephine realised immediately that the sudden boost given to those Mayan towns was the trigger that causes the riots in Quetzaltenango and San Salvador. The two British women realised that the situation was far from over.
'I told Rensy that Fiona was bad news!'
'Are you blaming this all on her? She was not the one that donated all that cash.'

[32] In today's money €3.187.500
[33] In today's money €573.750

‘The first sum of cash was donated by that chieftain. The second dose was on her request. The first dose already triggered people… the second those became too much.’
‘So, you are telling me that Mauro’s donations were a blessing… but that Fiona turned it into a curse by getting him to go over the top?’
‘Indeed…’
‘I agree… the 50.000 was already shocking enough… but the additional 40.000...’
‘People do not know the exact numbers…’
‘No… but the impact… that is what I am talking about.’
‘Well, this shows me that Fiona is successful. She not only got the attention of a wealthy chieftain. She also has such an influence on him that he spends much of his cash on strangers just to please her.’
‘However, her success comes with side-effects on the community. Four people died… now, those people had violent tendencies already. However, those four people are mourned by their relatives and now there is new bitterness against the Mayans that live remotely. So, on the long term… Fiona’s influence causes harm.’
‘I agree with you!’
‘It will not be long before people turn on her.’
‘Well, people were turning on her… it was then that she moved out of the public eye by going to Masaya… now, she is out of the public sight again… somewhere in a village in the rainforest.’
‘She is better off over there…’
‘What surprises me is that Balduno is so calm about all of this.’
‘Over forty-two days, Fiona’s extended Presidency will be over. He will be out of his job soon. He can just move to Sicily or to the United States, or wherever, after this.’
‘I think he is already preparing for his departure…’
‘Whoever succeeds Fiona will have a lot of headache to deal with.’
‘Have you seen Huyên?’
‘She moved to the village together with Fiona.’
‘Hmm… smart move. She has a friend with her over there.’
‘Did anyone find out who killed Hector?’
‘The last thing I heard was that he was assassinated by a hitman. They arrested some suspect that lives in Oaxaca.’
‘Well, quite some weird things are going on around here.’
‘You remember that weird French guy we saw months ago?’
‘Yeah…’

'He appears to have been involved in trafficking women into prostitution. He has been banned from Guatemala for five years. I found out that he was banned from the Viceroyalty of New Granada as well as the Captaincy General of Venezuela.'
'Well, be glad he is gone...'
'Five years is too little.'
'I know...'
'Where can we find Fiona now?'
'I think she is attending a meeting on Roatán Island this week.'
'Well, the timing is good.'
'Maybe we should join her...'
'We are not invited...'
'We do not need an invitation... we will just be sojourners that accidently pass by.'
'Then when is the meeting taking place?'
'Saturday morning.'
'It is Wednesday now...'
'We might make it if we depart now.'
'Good!'
While the two British friends look for a chariot to drive them to the Caribbean shores, Fiona, Huyên, Kandate, Kathura, Naomi, Aya, and Anna sang hymns together on the small ship that transferred them to Roatán. Mauro was in the 'captain's office' in the rear, while his wives did their chores on the ship. The small ship was given to Mauro in 1796 by several pirates who 'retired' from their criminal career. Mauro used the ship to sail on the Chamelecón River as well as the waters around the three 'Spanish' islands: Roatán, Utila and Guanaja. The meeting Mauro was on his way to be a meeting between several Black chiefs concerning how to deal with the political challenges that afflicted them as black confederacies in the empires of the Spanish and the British. Such meetings are done every half year. The location is often somewhere at the Caribbean shores of Central America.
Besides, Mauro and his wives, there were also three nuclear families on the ship. Those were some of the 'noble' families of Mauro's Confederacy. There were eight chieftains that would come to discuss economics and their plans for coming half year. It was the custom that each chieftain would bring his family with him. Due to Mauro's extended family being big, his children travelled separately several days earlier.

Huyên, by now, spoke Spanish almost fluently. She also befriended all of her co-wives since moving to Mauro's village.
'How long will it take before we arrive?'
'We will be leaving the mainland within an hour and from there it will take just a day before we arrive at Roatán. It will be a beautiful sight.'
'I just hope there is no strong wind on the Caribbean.'
'Even if there is... It is likely at the Antilles... not over here. We are close to the mainland.'
'Good.'
'You are from Asia, right?'
'Yeah...'
'Your Spanish is quite good.'
'Thanks, I learned it from hanging around Fiona.'
'Now that we mention her... where is she?'
'I have no clue...'
'Just check it out... we are about to eat some biscuits.'
'All right!'
Huyên walked around deck looking for her friend. Then she found her, at the Captain's office, standing in the half-open door. She wore a white short dress.
'Ey... what are you doing?'
'I am going to Mauro...'
'We are about to eat the biscuits.'
'Save some for me... I will be there later.'
'Are you up to something?'
'Just some favour I want from our man. See ya!'
'Bye...'
Huyên went back and she told the others that Fiona was with Mauro.
'Hmm... I wonder what she is up to.'
'She is kind of clogged to him.'
'Well, she is kind of in a honeymoon now.'
'Well... maybe it is because she has no children to look after'
'Her daughter is taken cared off at the village...'
'Hmm... she asked him to donate another 40.000 to the foundation where she worked... what else will she be asking of him?'
'Come on, girls... she is just new... just like Huyên.'
'Huyên is quite social with all of us... she is kind of withdrawing herself from the rest of us.'
'She might be a bit shy...'

‘Hmm…’
The women were not antagonistic against Fiona, but Fiona’s introvert behaviour kind of upset them. Huyên moved amongst them as if they have known each other for years.
‘Ey Huyên… why do you not go and check out what Fiona is discussing with him?’
‘Spying on them?’
‘Yeah…’
‘Well, all right… but remember… she does not speak English and he cannot speak Spanish… so there will not be much for them to communicate about.’
‘I will check’
Huyên moves slowly towards the window on deck of the Captain’s office. She then slowly opened the door and moved into the room. Around the corner, she saw Fiona kneels towards the rear window, while receiving backshots from her partner. Huyên closed the door to prevent the sound of Fiona’s voice from going throughout the ship. After several minutes, Mauro lay down, while Fiona was gasping for air. She opened the window ajar to get some fresh air. There was a little wind outside that blew the ship towards the Caribbean Sea. Fiona then sat at the open window and she starred. She just starred.
‘Mauro… I think we are being followed.’
Mauro did not respond.’
‘Hold on… I forgot… you do not speak Spanish…’
For a moment, she considered what to do. She then spoke in a Mayan language: ‘Darling, someone is following us.’
‘What did you say?’
Huyên was surprised that Mauro understood what Fiona said. Huyên did not understand anything they were saying.
‘You just spoke in a Mayan tongue.’
‘It is one of the Mayan languages that we use to interact with our base.’
‘Well, you are good at it.’
‘Where did you learn this Mayan language, Mauro?’
‘I learned it while studying in an English library.’
‘You can read and write English?’
‘Of course!’
‘Well, we found a way to communicate.’
‘I will learn Spanish soon. Do not worry.’
‘Well, I was telling you… I think we are being followed.’

‘What makes you think that?’
‘Come and see!’
Mauro looked out of the window and he saw three tiny ships coming after them.
‘You see?’
‘I do feel a bit chilly with them… but we do not know for sure whether they are following us.’
‘Do you have arms?’
‘Like a gun?’
‘Yes…’
‘I have three rifles and two guns on this ship.’
‘Give me a rifle.’
‘What?’
‘Give it to me, darling!’
‘Get it yourself… it is under this bed. The ammunition is on the nightstand.’
Fiona grabbed the rifle and the ammunition immediately.
‘You know how this works?’
‘Better…’, she picked up a beer bottle and placed it in front of the vent, ‘I know how to handle it.’
‘What are you doing?’
‘With the bottle stuck at the vent, she fired three shots with the rifle.’
‘What are you doing, woman?’
‘I am giving them warning shots… and I used a bottle to isolate the sound. That is why I fired after each other. Almost nobody heard the shots.’
‘Put that thing down!’
‘Fine’, she put in down on the bed, ‘At least now, they got the message.’
‘Are you crazy?’
‘We need to be sure that they are not coming to harm us.’
Mauro put the gun as well as the ammunition away.
‘What if they fired back?’
‘They did not…’
‘Do not do this again.’
‘Fine, my love’, she kissed him, ‘I will not!’
Huyên was shocked by what she just witnessed.
‘Another thing, we only speak Mayan when it is us two together. I do not want the others to know you speak Mayan.’

'That is fine… I will keep my mouth shut.'
'Good!'
'Hmm… Mauro!'
'Yeah?'
'What can I expect coming days?'
'Me and eight other chieftains will discuss our strategy on how to secure our interests for our fellow Black folks here in Central America and the Caribbean.'
'This is an illegal meeting?'
'It is not illegal… but it is a secretive meeting. So, only chieftains and their households, and some of their nobles, can be there.'
'Well, I kind of will be the odd one over there… the pale Spanish woman together with your dark-skinned wives.'
'Well, you are part of the household now… so will be my seed that will grow in your womb soon.'
'I hope so…'
'Tell me about the father of your daughter.'
'He is from a criminal background. His family comes from Matagalpa…'
'How did you get involved with him.'
'I met him during on of my speeches over there… and we met at a library and we have carnal knowledge.'
'Hmm… he left you with the child.'
'He disappeared and then he appeared later… wanting to see his child. He does not want me.'
'Hmm…. What did you do?'
'Well, I was in some difficult situations lately.'
'That is not what I asked…'
'It is the answer… the considered my family to be to toxic for him to put up with.'
'Are they toxic?'
'Yes… they are.'
'Are they still coming after us?'
Fiona looked outside the window.
'No…'
'I guess you were right then!'
'Trust me… I did whatever I could to keep Rensy close. However, I think I am better of without him.'
'Or… he is better of without YOU.'

'Why would you say that?'
'I felt after you moved into my village… that you had a foul spirit following you. One of my people did some ritual to keep the foul spirit at bay.'
'Oh….', she was shocked by hearing this, 'Thanks! I guess!'
'You remain close to me and you do not say A WORD without my permission, understood?'
'Yes, Sir!'
'Good! Now, close the window… it is a bit chilly outside!'
'Good!'
After she closed the window, she stood up and she inspected the room.
'What are you doing?'
'I just thought I saw someone around here…'
'You need some more physical affection I see…'
'Yeah', she kneeled again facing the window, 'Come keep me company!'
Huyên kept her mouth shut about what she witnessed. She did not want to cause any controversy on the ship. She did not understand a word that Mauro and Fiona exchanged. She went to the sleeping cabin to get some sleep after eating some of the biscuits.
The next morning, Fiona had a bad dream. She woke up with chills on her back, despite that it was warm inside the Captain's office. She looked outside of the window and she noticed that the mainland was almost invisible to her. She walked to the side window and she could see an island near the ship. She knew that it was not their place of destination. She put on a warm blanket and she walked towards one of the elder men who was already awake.
'Sir, what is that island?'
'That is Utila Island… we need to be at Roatán. It will take likely five to seven more hours before we arrive there.'
'Ah….'
'We have sailed this route often. It is familiar for us. How is the chief doing?'
'He is fine… he is still tired.'
'It will be a long week.'
'I am curious to meet the other chieftains. This is way more interesting than having performances with the Foundation.'
'About the Foundation, have you arranged your successor already?'
'He will be selected by the local donors. That is out of my hand.'

‘Hmm…. As long as it does not interfere with your duties over here.’
‘It will not.’
‘By the way, we will be going to Saint Elena, that is a sub-island of Roatán.’
‘As long as we are not hijacked by any pirates, I am happy.’
‘I grew up in Saint Vincent… my father was a slave imported from Negroland. When I was nineteen, I joined a rebellion and I moved – with my family – towards Guatemala. Mauro’s father passed away while trading on behalf of his slaveowner, in Santo Domingo. Ever since, the then 16-year-old Mauro was determined to set up his own tiny country. He married a 17-year-old black slave, from Saint Vincent and he had many children. When he moved towards Guatemala, he was thirty-nine and he had five wives already. He started his ‘nation’ in 1790 and in 1791 his government was established somewhere in the West of Spanish Honduras. Now, ten years later… he is a half-century old and one of the wealthiest chieftains in the Caribbean.’
‘He is a success!’
‘He surely is… he is not the only one. He only deals with other successful Blacks like himself.’
‘Why is that?’
‘It is not wise to deal with people who consistently failed at life… it is one thing to face tragedy, it is another thing if you are the tragedy yourself.’
‘I get it…’
‘You know Palenque?’
‘I heard about it. It is a free state somewhere in the Viceroyalty of New Granada… the Spanish Crown agreed to permit the kingdom to exist, as long as they would not accept new runaway slaves.’
‘They still do! Palenque sent an ambassador to this meeting.’
‘I am curious…’
‘About?’
‘How you all manage to keep this going without the colonial navies shutting it down.’
‘The colonial navies cannot even shut down piracy, let alone us. We are the least of their troubles!’
‘My dad owns a dukedom.’
‘We know… near Guayaquil. That is a bit isolated from all the trade.’
‘You got that right. He is often frustrated with his isolated position.’
‘Well, maybe you can relief him with the prosperity of Mauro.’

'I am not sure about that. I have not even informed him about this. None of my family. Truth being told, I will not inform them either. I do not feel comfortable disclosing so much about myself to them anymore.'
'What made you change your mind.'
'Well, let me say that my relatives used me to bail themselves out of trouble…'
'Ah!'
'That is why!'
'In any case, there is something else you need to know.'
'What is that?'
'The Mosquito Coast is a rival-kingdom towards Mauro and the two other Black chiefs in Spanish Honduras.'
'Why is that?'
'The Mosquito Indians want to retain their independence from Spanish Rule, and they still resist integrating in Spanish society. They instead want to unify with the chieftains of Honduras, both Zambo and Blacks, to form a confederacy under their Mosquito Rule.'
'Why do the Zambo and Black leaders in Spanish Honduras not just join them?'
'That would mean an open rebellion against Spain. Furthermore, the Zambo and Black chieftains contribute a lot to the Spanish economy in Guatemala. Spain needs us… so, why would we risk losing that leverage and all the benefits that come along with it.'
'Will there be a Mosquito Ambassador?'
'No… the Mosquito people are not willing to negotiate for autonomy under Spain.'
'I do not think that is a smart move.'
'Well, nobody can convince those folks… meanwhile, the Zambo and Blacks want to keep and increase their economic relevancy in Guatemala… that is the only way we can prevent our people from being crushed by slavery. Many Blacks are freed from slavery yearly and they join one of these communities. Many freed Blacks in Guatemala are working as local mercenaries for the Spanish Navy as well as transporters here in Honduras.'
'Hmm….'
'So, as a queen-consort of Mauro you will be requested to keep your eyes open for our interest.'

'I am… that is why I am not informing any of my relatives. I let them think I moved to the United States or something like that.'
'Good!'
'Why are we carrying the Spanish flag?'
'By carrying that flag, we will be left alone by foreign ships. That flag offers us legal protection worldwide.'
'Got it!'
While they still spoke, Huyên came and dragged Fiona away.
'We will talk later!'
Huyên pulled her to the galley. The galley was small and there were many ingredients stocked there.
'Huyên…'
'I heard you talking to Mauro when I came to bring some biscuits.'
'Talking?'
'What language was that?'
'Ehm…'
'There is no use in hiding it, Fiona…'
'It is a Mayan language.'
'Hmm… that explains it.'
'Just keep it between us…'
'My mouth is shut…'
'Good. I am getting used to this lifestyle. This also gives me an excuse to remain in Guatemala.'
'Me too!'
'By the way, he was asking about you.'
'Then when we arrive on the island, I will accompany him. You did your job well past days.'
'Hahahah….'
'By the way… I found out something odd.'
'What is it?'
'There has been riots.'
'Riots? Where?'
'Quetzaltenango and San Salvador… the money Mauro donated to the Mayan towns caused a violent reaction from many of the civilians.'
'Why are they so upset?'
'Well, first… Mauro is a black man… that is one thing and secondly, those Mayan towns were used as a dark motivation to keep other communities in line.'

'Well, nobody knows its Mauro that donated. The donors are never mentioned.'
'In any case… people have begun a witch-hunt to find out who the donor is. If they find out it is Mauro, we can face some serious retaliation.'
'IF they ever find out… which they will not!'
'I am glad your Presidency is over soon!'
'Me too…'
'What will Mauro do with the rest of the oil?'
'It is his oil now… so, it is none of my concern… nor yours.'
'Got it!'
'Let us get some breakfast. I cannot wait to be on land again… to take some shower at some spring.'
'There are still biscuits left… and some cold tea.'

13

Later that day, Balduno selected several candidates that could succeed Fiona. He handed his list of candidates to the notary officer in the capital. When he was about to go to his office, he encountered Rensy.
'Dude, what are you doing here?'
'I wanted to see my little girl.'
'Well, Fiona is not married to someone else.'
'What?'
'Well, it is not really a marriage… but she is now living with Maawiya II, a chieftain in the west of Spanish Honduras. He has his capital somewhere north of Copán. Gabrielle is there too.'
'I need to know where…'
'I think it is called Maawiya Town. But you will not find it on any official map.'
'I will ask around for it.'
'Have you seen Brittany and Josephine?'
'I did not…'
'I have not seen them either. My gut instinct tells me that they are in some type of dangerous situation.'
'Did she talk about the receipt?'
'I hope not…'
'Where was the last time you saw them?'
'Here at the Foundation. I heard them talking about sailing to Roatán.'
'What for?'
'I did not ask… It did not concern me.'
'Hmm… then figure out what is going on with Roatán.'
'I am on it… I think it is some Zambo feast that happens there every half year.'
'Zambo feast… and they want to attend? They are nuts!'
'Well, I figured that out a while ago. And Rensy, I would not just arrive uninvited at that village. Maawiya, or Mauro, is not fond of your unmanly behaviour. Any complaint from Fiona might trigger him, or his household, to kill you.'
'I will be watchful!'
Rensy walked away. He got on his horse to ride towards Copán immediately. When Balduno walked into the Foundation, a naval officer stopped him.
'Sir?'

'Are you Balduno Casighari?'
'Yes, Sir.'
'I am Tomás Gonzales. I am a lieutenant-officer appointed in the Bay of Honduras. I have some questions for you.'
'Come to my office.'
The office was clean and decorated in a simple manner. The two men sat down.
'What can I do for you?'
'Maawiya Ifuntade, also known as Chief Mauro, has donated a sum of 90.000 Spanish Dollars to this foundation. Am I correct?'
'Sir…'
'I have a warrant from the admiral to interrogate you.'
The officer showed the warrant.
'Yes, Mister Ifuntade did donate such amount of money.'
'Sources told me… that Fiona Rodrigues has become a concubine of this chieftain after the first sum of transaction. Correct?'
'Well… they are sexually involved. Yes.'
'So, the first donated sum was more a bride price in disguise…'
'Well, bride price to whom?'
'To Spanish society. Mauro is bailing himself out by unofficially marrying a Spanish criolla to give more legitimacy to his confederacy. By sponsoring the Mayan towns near the Pacific, he also won allies. He is smart. We cannot deny that.'
'Then… what is the issue?'
'The riots that emerged in San Salvador caused a political drama in Mexico City. The viceroy is incredibly angry about this!'
'Look, it is not my fault that the public could not handle some disadvantaged people receiving some generosity.'
'Balduno… you know how politics work!'
'That is why I am not a politician. So, what do you want?'
'Do you know Jacques-Marie Toulon?'
'Hmm…. that does not right a bell.'
'The same man who has been banned, for five years, from entering Venezuela, New Granada as well as Guatemala. He has been seen various times with you. He is involved in trafficking women from Guatemala and Venezuela towards French brothels. Furthermore, he is rumoured to have been covered by you.'
'What makes you think that Sir?'

'It does not matter what I think, young man. What matters is that your name is cleared.'
'What do YOU want, Sir?'
'Fiona, now renamed Fayola by her host community, is attending a conference on Saint Elena, a tiny island that is part of Roatán Island.'
'So… what has that to do with me?'
'Do you know what her agenda is?'
'Agenda?'
'Look, Balduno… she knew that a chieftain was about to visit the Foundation after she declined to attend his wedding. Later, you find out that she was the one expected to be the bride. Why did she just give in so easily?'
'I am not sure if you are aware… but last year has been horrible on her. Her fiancée left her after their baby was born, she was suspected of involvement in a political double homicide, her aunt went missing and she was found dead months later, her half-uncle whom she never knew was murdered… so, give her some leeway. Please. She did not commit treason.'
'So, there is no way this is related to the fact that the Dominguez Household is suing her relatives for extortion?'
'What?'
'A court order, from a judge in Seville, placed her uncle Lionel… under house arrest. Lionel Rodrigues took advantage of the financial distress of the Dominguez Household to cover up his sabotage of various local investments in South America. Philemon Dominguez was considering abolishing the whole Foundation and to start a trade-union together with the Zambo and Black Confederacies in Central America and the Caribbean.'
'I had no clue about that…'
'Did she have contact with her relatives?'
'Barely… they were not on good term with her, Sir.'
'Hmm….'
'So, you think Fiona is plotting something?'
'Or… someone is using her to plot something.'
'Mauro?'
'Or… Mauro's people. We just want to be alert, so we know when to intervene.'
'Leave those blacks alone man… they do not harm any of Guatemala's interests.'

‘No… but they do attract unnecessary enemies from the other side of the Caribbean and that is our concern.’
‘This foundation is not involved with any political project. We are strictly interested in helping disadvantages Mayan towns.’
‘That will not be needed soon… now those Mayan towns are going through an economic revival… thanks to… Fiona.’
‘The moment I hear something, I will inform you.’
‘Not needed… we have people around Roatán informing us daily. Thanks for your cooperation.’
‘Yes, Sir!’
At that moment, Mauro’s ship arrived at Saint Elena where Mauro’s children were awaiting him. After getting to land, the concubines were led to a tiny village with many accommodations. Mauro would remain with the other chieftains, separately. Fiona met the children of Mauro, as well as the children of the other chieftains. She was the only pale woman around, which made her the spectacle of the evening.
The next morning, the chieftains and the ‘elders’ they brought with them held their first meeting. The first challenge they discussed was the increase of British pirates who sought to sabotage the income of the confederacies.
‘Look brothers, we need to be firm in this: our households and our people depend on our commerce going well.’
‘We know that.’
‘That is why we must form a front against their annoying pirates.’
‘Many of those pirates are backed up by the British Navy… good luck with defeating them.’
‘We do not have to defeat them if we can join them.’
‘What are you talking about, Maawiya?’
‘What do those pirates want?’
‘They want some of the bounty of Spanish America…’
‘So, we give it to them… on the condition that they watch over our interests.’
‘What makes you think this will work on our favour?’
‘If we manage to get those British pirates in the Caribbean on our side… we will calm down many of their attacks on Spanish ports. That will increase the confidence of the Spanish Crown in our usefulness. That will grant us more economic relevancy and even political relevancy in Spanish America. We already have economic relevancy. We need to increase it at all costs…’

'That white woman you just married, is she an asset too?'
'She is one of my wives and she is an asset… I only sleep and live with assets. Hoes I execute!'
'How will you use her, and that Asian wife of yours, in our favour?'
'Fiona already benefited us by conceding her inheritance to me…'
'Inheritance?'
'I wanted to purchase some Asian oil from this mestizo… from The Philippines. Later, I find out he was murdered… and that he left all his oil, in Costa Rica, to his niece. I find out who this niece is, through Maduro. Maduro informed me of how well-behaved and physically beautiful she was… I was also informed that she had an equally beautiful servant, from Asia. So, me and Maduro made a calculated plan… I invest in the Mayans to get them on our side… and I will gain both two new wives… good for more offspring… and I will gain the Asian oil. Maduro came with the plan to sell the oil four times the original price… to earn more profit. He got away with it… so… my household, as well as my confederacy, increased five-fold in riches in less than a week.'
'Wow!'
'So… I knew what I was doing when marrying Fiona, and Huyên.'
'Will you expand to Asia too?'
'That is the point. That is where we are heading!'
'Good…'
'What about the Mosquito Kingdom?'
'Those guys will not bend…'
'Their determination is honourable… but it is also foolish. They need to be flexible with the Spaniards.'
'They will never be convinced of that!'
'Well, we should leave them alone for now… we must focus on our expansion.'
While the men continued their conference, Fiona walked on the beach with her fellow concubines and the wives of the other chieftains. The women spoke Spanish and English with one another. The atmosphere was good. She enjoyed the company of those other people.
After four days, the conference was ended, and the group held a big feast where the women danced for the men. It was the first time Fiona twerked and she did it quite well. She was surprised herself.

14

The morning when each of them was about to depart to their homes, a small ship arrived on Saint Elena. It was a tiny vessel with nobody else than Brittany and Josephine on it. Fiona recognised them immediately.
'Hey Brit… Josephine… what are you doing here?
'We were checking on you.'
'By following me?'
'We have something to tell you…'
'Not now… I just had a great time.'
'What did you do?'
'There was a conference here… it is over. I had a great time.'
'Anyway…'
'Wait till we are back on the Spanish Main…'
'All right.'
Fiona walked away with her co-wives. Brittany and Josephine decided to do what Fiona said. That evening, Mauro's children departed on their ship and Mauro departed on his ship with the rest of his household. Josephine and Brittany sailed side by side with Mauro's ship all the way to the delta of the Chamelecón River. Josephine and Brittany followed Mauro's household all the way back to their main village.
At the main village, however, there was a surprise that awaited Mauro: a small battalion of 400 infantry, under the lead of Tomás Gonzales awaited him.
Mauro commanded his children and his wives, except Fiona and Huyên, to silently ride to another village. Mauro, Fiona and Huyên approached Lieutenant Gonzales who awaited at Mauro's villa.
'Mister Oguntade…'
'Lieutenant Gonzales y Domas. What can I do for you?'
'Can we talk alone?'
'Just for a little moment.'
Huyên and Fiona moved into the villa, while Mauro sat down near the lieutenant.
'So, what is going on now?'
'I see you enriched yourself with two new brides.'
'Well, as a king I need to show ambition.'
'Well, Guatemala already has a king…'
'Who lives across the Atlantic Ocean, in the middle of the Iberian Peninsula. I am not contending for the throne of Guatemala… I just

have my own community over here and we want to be stable and self-sufficient… not dependent on Spain for anything.'
'I agree with you…'
'I need to stand for my own people… nobody else will.'
'That is why I am surprised you chose that criolla as a new bride.'
'All my first five wives were from my same background… now, I got one from the land of our captivity and one from an exotic kingdom in the east… I do not see the problem here.'
'Well, her father might be. Her father is not fond of negroes nor those mixed with negroes.'
'Well, she is sleeping with one now and soon she will give birth to a Negro baby.'
'Well, that will trigger war against you.'
'Where is her father now?'
'Somewhere in Quito…'
'Well, he is likely to stay there… with all the problems he is facing right now. So, he is no threat to me.'
'Just be prepared… the Rodrigues Household can be quite vengeful.'
'Look, lieutenant… if my people were vengeful, we would have shut down Guatemala's trade completely by burning down all the ports at its Caribbean shores. WE did not… we just demanded to have some land and space to have our own lives at peace and we voluntarily pay taxes to His Majesty, Charles IV. So… we are really an ally of Spain.'
'Well, the ministers and the king will see you like this… but the criollos will never admit that.'
'The criollos need us… it is us keeping British pirates at bay. Without us… Guatemala would collapse, and the rebel-Indians would commit arson and riots all over the place.'
'You are very strategic.'
'So, should you be!'
'When my military service is over, I expect to retire somewhere in Cuba or in Yucatan.'
'You do not want to settle down in Spain itself?'
'Nope! Never! I want the Caribbean climate as well as the lifestyle of this warm place. I prefer to be around the tribes mixed with negros than to be around my own xenophobic people.'
'Where is your wife?'
'She just gave birth to our fourth son. Jaimy.'

‘Good! You have accomplished a lot and you married the woman you wanted, not who your family wanted you to be with.’
‘It came with a high price…’
‘Well, doing what is best often is…’
‘Can you do me a favour?’
‘What is it?’
‘There is a group of criollos, near Masaya, that are looking for an occasion to get me locked up.’
‘Why?’
‘I stopped them from scapegoating several mestizo boys in San Miguel. So, now they have filled in reports against me, and I might be called to give an account before the Viceroy.’
‘That is off…’
‘I have an awfully bad feeling about this.’
‘So, do I… I think I can handle this for you. Is it Moreila’s gang that is behind this?’
‘They are…’
‘Those creeps even attempted to pay some Mosquito hitmen to come and assassinate some of my men… but the Mosquito diplomats even came here and informed me.’
‘Hmm… he does not give up.’
‘When will you go home again?’
‘I will be home tonight… at Santo Tomás de Castilla.’
‘Good… spend time with your wife. Leave the rest to me!’
‘Good!’
The lieutenant, and his battalion, left Mauro’s village.
After this, Maduro approached the chief about the departing Spanish soldiers.
‘Do not worry, Mamadu, he just asked for a favour.’
‘How many favours does he need? He needs to go to his own people for that.’
‘We got his back… he got ours.’
‘What does he need?’
‘I think it is time to shut down the Moreila gang.’
‘If we get involved with this…’
‘We are not getting involved… we are preventing the Moreila’s from attacking our people again and while we do that, we also help our Mister Gonzales.’
‘I got it…

‘Well, you can gather twenty men and if needed, recruit some guys from Nicaragua too, and do what you have to do.’
‘How far?’
‘No need to kill anyone… just shut their operation down, FOR GOOD!’
‘Understood!’
After Maduro left, Mauro entered his house where Fiona awaited him.
‘What was that?’
‘Nothing you have to worry about.’
‘Well,’, she embraced him, ‘Good to hear that!’
‘Keep out of the problems that afflict my tribe… I, and Maduro, will deal with those. Get more acquainted with my children and with the women of our community.’
‘I liked the party we held at Saint Elena.’
‘There will be more of such parties… but this is not just partying. There are also concerns you need to be involved in…’
‘I got it!’
‘What about those two white women?’
‘Oh… Josephine and Brittany?’
‘They had something they wanted to tell me… so, they looked up where I was.’
‘Go and talk to them. I will be spending some time with Huyên.’
‘Hahaha… fine. I will let you know what they said.’
‘Good!’
Fiona left the house, and she approached her two British associates.
‘So, what was it that you came to talk to me about?’
‘Do you remember those two detectives that approached you about that shooting in Nicaragua?’
‘Wait…’
‘Where you met Rensy… there was a shooting.’
‘O yeah… that is a while ago!’
‘They filled another report about you… you are being suspected of misappropriation of funds from the foundation.’
‘What?’
‘Well, that is what we wanted to tell you… it is better for you to stay away from the Foundation for a while… or better, away from Guatemala City.’
‘Good for informing me…’
‘How is it to be a Zamba-queen?’
‘Well… it is fun… it is exciting.’

‘Is there some place for us here?’
‘What do you mean?’
‘We would like to live here for a while…’
‘You can.’
‘Just tell Mauro that we will be helping you out. We speak English and we can teach you it too.’
‘That is a great idea!’
‘I will tell him later… right now, he is mating with Huyên.’
‘You spoiled him the first several days, I guess.’
‘Yeah, absolutely!’
‘Have you heard from Rensy?’
‘No… I do not even need to hear from him.’
‘He is the father of Gabrielle.’
‘He will have to talk to Mauro if he wants to see Gabrielle. Is he coming here?’
‘I am not sure he even knows where this village is.’
‘That is better! Anyway, let us get some seasoned chicken… later we will talk with Mauro and you girls can move in with me.’
The three women caught some fish from the river, and they baked them after seasoning them with cumin and salt. As drinks, Fiona bought some mango juice from an elderly woman.
When sunset approached, the three women joined the other women in the village and they began to sing African songs, including two songs in Portuguese. While they were singing, Mauro approached Fiona and he give a thumbs up… while pointing to Josephine and Brittany. Fiona understood immediately that it was Huyên that already negotiated to keep the two British associates in the village.
That evening, Josephine and Brittany moved into Fiona’s room. Fiona went away, into the rainforest, to gaze at the stars. Despite that Mauro warned her not to wander off too much into the forest, due to human traffickers that were lurking around. After two hours, she went back inside, and she went beneath her blankets.
‘You went stargazing again?’
‘Yeah… as I always do.’
‘Well, next time we want to join you.’
‘Just do not let Mauro find out. He will be upset I went into the rainforest so late.’
‘We are close to the border with the District of Amatique?’
‘Yeah… we are.’

'It feels like Amatique and Honduras are two different nations all together. The closer to Guatemala City you come, the more you know the 'real' Guatemalans… and the more away from the capital, the more the people form their own communities and their own identities.'
'Some even doubt whether Costa Rica should remain part of Guatemala… the people down there do not even feel a direct connection to Guatemala City.'
'Well, till Nicaragua… I can say… they are all Guatemalans. But the people in Honduras…'
'They are darker…'
'Yeah, that is one.'
'And they are more open to what goes on in the rest of the world. I feel like many of the people at the Pacific side of Guatemala are quite closed-off from the rest of the world.'
'Can you blame them? Their towns and cities are built close to the Pacific… the Spanish did this to make sure pirates of the Caribbean could not harm their colony. That is why they developed into an isolated people within the empire.'
'Got it…'
'Anyway, let us go to sleep. We have a big day tomorrow!'
What Josephine and Brittany told Fiona was old news: the detectives were already removed from the case for almost a month. The case was declared 'cold' on the instruction of a colonial offer in Seville who oversaw the criminal cases of the Province of Nicaragua. The colonial officer was not happy with the fact that a criolla was around a fatal gang shooting, especially when he found out that the criolla involved was Fiona Rodrigues.
While Fiona, and her British housemates, were sleeping, that same colonial officer held a small meeting in Seville, discussing the situation in Nicaragua concerning the Matagalpa Indians. At the meeting there were two Roman Catholic clerks, five administrators and a general.
'Gentlemen, thank you for being here… this early morning.'
'You're welcome, Diego!'
'Listen, the reason I wanted you all to come was to discuss the dire situation in Guatemala, particularly in the Province of Nicaragua.'
'Does this relate to the Mosquito Coast?'
'No… we have a whole panel in Cadiz dealing with that already. This has to do wit the Matagalpa Area.'
'Hmm… what has happened now?'

'There was a public shooting and it happened near a library in Matagalpa, there was also a criolla nearby when it happened. Apparently, she was in a sexual relationship with one of the suspects.'

'Who is this criolla?'

'Fiona Rodrigues, the niece of Lionel Rodrigues.'

'Is that the businessman whose wife was just killed in Guatemala?'

'Well, just killed… it has been a while now. She went missing there and she was found dead.'

'How did she end up there?'

'Likely, they had marital problems… or whatever… what matters is that this Fiona is also the President of the Santa Barbara Foundation in Guatemala City… and there have been some interesting developments over there also.'

'Like what?"

'A sudden donation of 50.000 Spanish Real from a British migrant that lives in the Province of Honduras. We do not know that much about him, apart that he is Black and that he has a lot of money.'

'Hmm… what is this man's name?'

'He is called *Maawiya Oguntade*. He has the Spanish alias Mauro. He has a small military force of around 200 men, and he lives in the West of Honduras.'

'Two hundred men… that is not something to be afraid of.'

'Well, Mister Oguntade… has an estimated wealth of 2.000.000 Spanish Real[34]… which makes him the richest Black chieftain in the New World and one of the richest ex-slaves alive!'

'Hmm… 2.000.000… that is a lot!'

'What I am stating here is that we need to keep a firm eye on this Mauro… He might become a danger soon.'

'We surely need to prevent him from expanding.'

'Well, is it not the responsibility of the Royal Audiencia in Guatemala City to keep an eye on the provinces in Central America?'

'It is… however, Guatemala is a fragile area. Honduras contains much wealth, but also a lot of black power and foreign settlers. Nicaragua is quiet and stable, but there is much smuggling going on. Look, this Mauro lives in Honduras, but he can easily join forces with the Matagalpan gangs and if that happens, we might have a large-scale rebellion in Central America.'

'Hmm… does he have any enemies?'

---

[34] In today's money €12.750.000

'He has the Moreila Syndicate that smuggles much from South America, via Nicaragua, towards the United States.'
'Hmm… what is the conflict about?'
'The Mosquito Indians are opposed to the Moreilas… and Mauro supports them in it.'
'Ah… that is a volatile situation!'
'Realise… that the Moreilas, despite being corrupt, are the most reliable asset we have in maintaining a consistent revenue from Nicaragua and Costa Rica... they are also the main opposition against the Matagalpan rebellion that is still going on.'
'That is why we need to preserve the Moreilas… that means that we need to cut short the influence of this Mauro in Guatemala.'
'What is the best thing we have to restrain him.'
'What we can do… is send an order to the Royal Audiencia to block the roads in the West of Honduras… this will hinder his economy.'
'This will also hinder the common everyday transactions in Honduras too.'
'People can use other roads to do what they have to do.'
'Wait… if he is in the West of Honduras, why not place a naval blockade? We have several naval bases over there. Put a naval blockade and then you starve this guy out.'
'Hmmm…. that is a possibility.'
'A naval blockade is the cheapest… We just put ten extra ships on the two rivers that flow from near the Amatique-Honduras border and Mauro is finished.'
'Then we do that…'
'A naval blockade will also cost something. Who is going to pay all the sailors who have to conduct extra patrols?'
'The extra salary can be paid from the treasury of the Kingdom of Guatemala. Guatemala has experienced an increase in revenue in taxes past decade. So, it should not be a problem.'
'This is an issue that needs to be resolved locally. Our supervision must concern foreign policies and naval threats.'
'So… who votes for and who votes against a naval blockade?'
The attendees wrote down their decision on a piece of paper.
'Noes are two and Ayes are fifteen. That seals the matter.'
'What about that Santa Barbara Foundation? As far as I know, the Dominguez Family is constantly the target of controversies. What if this

Santa Barbara Foundation is just another one of their schemes to remain off the hook of the judge?'
'If that is the case, they are failing miserably.'
'That Fiona is both involved with a low life from Matagalpa, and she is the President of a prestigious charity organisation? Something is amiss here!'
'She is the daughter of Gregorio Rodrigues, who as suspected of involvement in the murder of Felipe Victoria y Gazzette and Filemon de Montana y Valdes.'
'Was Gregorio's daughter not also a suspect at some point?'
'She was... but a later judge figured out that the suspicion was not grounded in convincing evidence.'
'So, we have two controversies in Nicaragua... a noble lady that shags up with a low-life criminal and a Black chieftain that is exercising political power without any formal recognition from His Majesty.'
'Correct...'
'So, let us deal with them both. Let us find out whether the duchess as well as the chieftain have anything in common.'
'What could they have in common?'
'Just to be sure, my gut feeling tells me that those two have more in common than we realise.'

15

The Royal Audiencia of Guatemala, just thirty-one days after the meeting concerning Nicaragua in Seville, received the order from the Council of the Indies to put a naval blockade on the rivers Chamelecón and Ulúa. The colonial officer in charge advised ten ships on the Chamelecón River, and eight ships on the Ulúa River. However, the vice-President of the Royal Audiencia did not agree with the order.
He arranged a meeting with the military department to discuss what could be done. The military ministers agreed with him. The group came with a compromise… five ships would be used to patrol the Chamelecón River and two ships on the Ulúa River to find out what was going on with the activities of Maawiya Oguntade.
A week later, the ships sailed on the rivers to check the river ports for activities relating to 'Mr. Oguntade'. Two months into the investigation, no strange activities were found. The local authorities, however, did find out that a woman named Fayola Oguntade bribed two customs officers in allowing tobacco into San Pedro Sula. It became clear that Fayola Oguntade was just an alias for the woman's real identity. By this time, Mauro often visited San Pedro Sula and Comayagua to arrange his financial affairs. There have been fiscal investigations into his finances twice and no foul play was discovered. According to the registry in Guatemala City, Mauro was unmarried and therefore he could not be charged with bigamy – despite that he was spotted with his multiple spouses in various occasions and despite that all his children were registered as his children. Mauro's eldest son, Jairo, purchased a small house in San Pedro Sula. He handed over receipts of his 'foreign service' in the British Navy, which could not be verified.
It was now four and a half months since Fiona exchanged her office at the Foundation for a room in Mauro's village. By now, Huyên was four months pregnant and Fiona's English skills increased. She was not able to write simple letters in English as well as expressing her emotions.
By now, Mauro got into an alliance with a Zambo importer from Paris. The Zambo importer was born in French Guyana to a Black slave father and a native slave girl. At age nineteen, the young man escaped to Surinam where he worked in the harbour for two years. After the years, in 1781, he boarded a ship to France where he started a new life as *Dean Jules*. Ever since, he has been importing produce of Zambo farmers living in the Viceroyalty of New Spain as well as the Captaincy

General of Venezuela. He did this to support as many Zambo households as possible. Dean, now forty years of age, spoke French and Spanish as if it were both his mother tongues. He also learned English over the years due to using British captains as middlemen. Dean was not a rich man, nor was he considered wealthy by the people in Paris.
Since the French Riots of the late 1780s and the chaos of the early 1790s, Dean began to focus more on Zambo exporters from Guatemala and Puerto Rico.
Dean, and his wife *Adrienne* (whose mother was a Black slave), agreed to sail to Guatemala to meet Mauro personally in his village. Maduro arranged a meeting between Mauro and Dean in Puerto de Caballos. Mauro decided he would meet Dean together with Fiona and Huyên.
Currently, Fiona and Huyên were preparing for the arrival of Dean and Adrienne which was likely to happen within less than a week. There was already a chariot ready to drive them to Puerto de Caballos the moment the message arrived that Dean arrived in Guatemala.
Fiona was excited to meet the French guest. Huyên was more focussed on baby names for her future child.
Josephine, by now, noticed something weird about Fiona's situation: Fiona was not even aware of the controversial position she was in! Brittany noticed the same thing, but she did not pay much attention to it.
Mike, at this time, resided in the city San Salvador together with another British migrant, Ilona. He decided to stay in Guatemala until 1805. There were felonies he committed whose Statute of limitations would expire in 1803. He wanted to remain an extra two years away just to be sure. He worked as a goldsmith and glassblower, and it brought him a stable income.
One day, Mike received Brittany's letter in which she informed him about the meeting between Mauro and Dean that was about to take place. Mike, however, felt uncomfortable about that meeting. He discussed the matter with several older people.
'So, young man… you are distressed about a meeting between two black men who seek to benefit each other?'
'There is something about this Dean guy… for some reason, reading about him alarmed me.'
'So, let us go through it… he is a former slave, who lived in France for a while and now he decided to leave Europe and to come to Guatemala.'

‘Indeed… and the thing about it is… why does he come to Guatemala? There is Puerto Rico, Saint-Domingue, Cuba, the Lucayans, Florida… there are many Black exporters over there too… This place is a bit isolated for him to come all the way here … to meet a man he does not know.’
‘That is weird, indeed!’
‘The meeting is likely to happen next week.’
‘Just let it happen, and your sister will inform you about how it works out. In case anything is off, she can always inform the local magistrates.’
‘True…’
‘Do not worry too much!’
Mike listened to the advice of the elderly and he let it go.
Four days later, a mailman arrived in Mauro’s village with news that ‘Mr. and Mrs. Jules’ arrived in Trujillo and that two days from then they will arrive in Puerto de Caballos. Mauro informed Fiona, Huyên and Maduro about the matter.
‘Two days from now… around three… midday… we will meet our brother at the port. Make sure that you are ready by then.’
‘Yes, Sir!’
‘And you, Fiona… we need to talk.’
‘Sure…’
He brought Fiona near a small fountain.
‘What is on? Darling?’
‘Do you know anyone named Juliette Robinsen?’
‘Hmm…. I do remember a girl with that name. It was when I was a little girl. Around eight years old. She attended the same grammar school as I did. In Guayaquil.’
‘Hmm…. she is Dean’s wife.’
‘What?’
‘He handed over a receipt of his arrival in Trujillo and here you can see her name’
‘*Juliette Daisy Robinsen*, born on the 16th of August 1780, Staffordshire, Great Britain.’
‘She married him just several months ago.’
‘When I was ten, Juliette’s parents moved back to Britain. Her parents were a diplomatic couple that were appointed to the Viceroyalty of New Granada on behalf of the British Governor of Jamaica.’
‘Hmm… now she is married to Dean.’

'Juliette's mother is from Africa, by the way.'
'I thought so…'
'Why did you ask if I knew her?'
'Maduro found out about your early childhood and he requested the receipts from the local churches in Quito.'
'He did a whole background check on me?'
'My household is the leading factor in this community. I do not risk any bad woman to have access to me.'
'I give you that…'
'I am more concerned with something else.'
'What is that?'
'That grammar school you attended… those children were all children of diplomats, missionaries as well as some high-ranking foreign mercenaries. I figured out that most of the children that attended that school, boys and girls, are either dead now… or they are missing.'
'What?'
'From 1789 till 1791, fifty-four children attended that school. From all of them, twelve are still confirmed alive. Other died of tragic accidents or they are gone…'
'That is weird.'
'So, my question is… where their weird things going on at that grammar school?'
'It was just a common Roman Catholic school for children from wealthy households. I did not notice any else that was weird. The principal of the school, however, often had 'favourite' children around him. Often boys.'
'Hmm…. I know enough.'
'What?'
'It is obvious that there was sexual misconduct towards some of the children over there…'
'Well…'
'Did it ever happen to you?'
'Me? Never! I was always at ease.'
'That is good. I have the idea that Dean might have been aware of my existence because of you.'
'Me?'
'Two months ago, I received a letter from Dean asking for a meeting. He gave me a whole report of his economic activities past years and how he plans to support Zambos and Blacks in Guatemala and Puerto

Rico. I thought it was kind of strange. However, I am open for allies… but I do want to know of my allies are real allies and not agents in disguise.'
'I have not been in contact with Juliette ever since age ten. I was not even aware she was in France now… let alone married tot this potential ally of ours.'
'Hmm… who do you think had contact with her?'
'The only ones that knew about Juliette were my uncles, who relied on that British diplomat for some benefits in Britain.'
'Ahhh…'
'Wait… you think that my deceased aint-in-law was keeping some correspondence with Juliette? I have no idea why she would do that. By the time I knew Juliette, she was not even with my uncle… I believe.'
'Your aunt-in-law was an agent that perished during her mission… and now it seems that another agent is activated in her place.'
'Agent for what?'
'That is what we will find out within two days.'
'Should I ask her?'
'No, pretend as if you are not aware of anything. It can be that my suspicion is false.'
'Your intuition is never false, Maawiya. We will find out what is going on, sooner or later. I hope sooner.'
'How is the father of your daughter?'
'He just came and visited her yesterday. Well, I am on good terms with him… but it is clear now that we will not be getting together anymore. Even if I was without a companion.'
'I am glad he got the message.'
'Did the situation with the Moreila's got resolved?'
'Trust me, the Moreila's will not be bothering us again!'
'Great. That means our children will be free from future retaliation.'
'We cannot guarantee the absence of future tribulation, but we can secure the present as far as we are able to.'
'Correct!'
'Did you contact your father?'
'No, I have not spoken to my parents for a while… and I do not intend to. They will turn on you, and this whole community, and then they will seek revenge. I have an address in San Pedro Sula, so they will think that I am living over there.'
'I have the same thing.'

‘Well, you need to have something to distract them.’
‘Then write letters as if you are living in San Pedro Sula. They need some insurance that you are well.’
‘You are right… I will write one today. Then my father will have it within a week, I suppose.’
‘You can let Maduro post it. He will be going to San Pedro Sula tonight.’
‘Why do we not become more active in the urban economy?’
‘It is too early or that… if we do that, the Spanish cartels might perceive us as a threat. Right now, we are the buffer between the Spanish cartels and the robbing foreign pirates… so, we must use that leverage to get what we want, indirectly.’
‘I get it!’
‘By the way, why did you accept the invitation to partake in the election for the Santa Barbara Foundation?’
‘Well, it was a way for me to stay away from my parents a bit longer. Furthermore, I liked the party-life in Guatemala City. Sometimes, we would even travel all the way to Quetzaltenango to get drunk… I wanted to keep that life for a while.’
‘That life would have only ended in tragedy.’
‘I see that now, and now that I have Gabrielle… I want to be more considerate of how my actions affect her.’
‘You did the right thing by keeping that man away from you.’
‘I do not even want him to be around her… but it is her father, so I cannot be so cruel. She is entitled to know who her father is.’
‘It is also his responsibility to become involved with her, not you. You do your part; he does his part. God will reward you.’
‘Amen!’
While they still spoke, a mail carrier arrived.
‘Mister Oguntade, you got mail!’
‘From whom is it?’
‘From the government.’
‘Oh dear… government.’
‘I know man, nobody loves the government.’
‘In any case, let us get this over with.’
‘You do not have to pay me… the government covered all the expenses.’
‘Ah… good!’
‘See you!’

'¡Gracias!'
'What is it about?', Fiona became interested, 'What does the government want from you?'
'Come and read it with me.'
'Hold on…'

Dear Mr. Maawiya Adebowale Oguntade,

As part of an annual inspection, we request all foreign residents from the continent of Africa to hand in accounts of their financial activities within the Intendancy of Honduras. You can report your activities within a month after receiving this letter at the address below the text of this letter. The receipts will be processed by our financial and judicial officers in the Commercial Office in Comayagua and later also by the Royal Chamber of Commerce in Guatemala City.

We thank you, in advance, for your cooperation.

Diego Damario y Valdes
Secretary of the Vice-intendant of Honduras

'Wow…'
'I do not fall for this.'
'Darling, they just want to have some receipt.'
'Fayola…'
'If you do not co-operate, they will get suspicious.'
'They are already suspicious. It is quite weird that after the increase of my wealth, after marrying you, that suddenly they become interested in my financial activities. It seems as if they are suspecting some type of criminal activity on my part. I am telling you; this is a set-up!'
'Not everything is a set-up darling, I was not.'
'No, you were my desire… this people, desire my death. There is nothing more abominable to them than a Black chieftain that outdoes the local Spanish cartels.'
'Cheer on… maybe this is a good sign.'
'We will see about that. Anyway, write your letter to your parents. After meeting with Dean… we will discuss this request of the government.'
'Right!'
Fiona wrote a long letter to her father, explaining how good she has been without informing him about her life in Mauro's village. She also put a little jewel in the letter as a gift for her mother.
'Maduro…'

'Fayola!'
'I got a letter for my father. Please, post it tonight when you arrive in San Pedro Sula.'
'I will do! Anything else, that is it!'
'Ma'am…'
'Yeah?'
'Do you trust Huyên?'
'Well, yeah…'
'Hmm… I notice she is becoming clingier with Maawiya lately.'
'Well, she is pregnant of him.'
'So, she is not about to become one of your rivals?'
'Hell no!'
'Good… just keep an eye on her. I feel she is a bit unstable.'
'Unstable?'
'Mentally…'
'Ah.'
'Just keep an eye on her.'
'I will!'
'¡Adios!'
From there, Fiona went to a waterfall to take another chilly shower. She loved taking chilly showers in the warm tropical weather. While she was showering, she reflected on everything that happened since the day she ventured with her former staff to Matagalpa. She realised that her life changed completely after that trip. She was doubting whether to go to Matagalpa to hold a meeting. However, the party-girl inside of her was curious about the party life in Nicaragua.
It was there that she met Rensy. It was there that she got pregnant. It was there that she become involved in a homicide investigation. It was from that point on, that she has been on a roller coaster ever since. She was glad that she was a mother now and she was glad that she managed to stay away from her parental house. She was glad to remain in Guatemala, the kingdom she was in love with. However, her fairy tale ease was about to be disrupted soon…

16

Maduro and Mauro stood at the port. They were awaiting the ship to arrive. It was now 14:30 and they expected the ship to arrive by now. Just ten metres away, was Huyên and Fiona in their colourful dresses. The two ladies were excited for the later afternoon.
'So, what do you expect that will come from this meeting?'
'Well, that depends.'
'On what?'
'Well, Huyên… I know Mauro a bit better now. He is overly cautious of forming allies. That is why he is happy that Dean wanted to meet him in person.'
'He comes all the way from France. That is a long trip!'
'Yeah… I would like to visit France soon.'
'I am not really into European countries. It is good enough that Europeans are occupying most of the earth's surface with their military.'
'Hahahah….'
'By the way, what happened to your cousins?'
'Well, my female cousins are still in Guatemala City. They have never left… however, since my relationship with Rensy they barely speak to me.'
'Hmmm… why is that?'
'Those female cousins, children and grandchildren of my uncles just wants to have a good time. They do not want to be involved in any political matters.'
'Why did your cousins not respond to the news of their mother-in-law being in Guatemala?'
'They cannot stand her.'
'Oh dear.'
'I guess they knew she was a cheater after all.'
'Did you find out anything else about this Luis de Aragon?'
'He is under investigation. I want to keep it at that. My life is in Guatemala and that means dealing with the challenges around here. It was a blessing in disguise for me that my half-uncle passed away. Not that I wished any bad on him. Due to his passing, I got the attention of Mauro and that is how I ended up here… with him… with you… on this beautiful warm day in Puerto de Caballos.'
'Well, I hope our lives remain as peaceful as it is now.'

'Why do you expect it to get worse?'
'Mauro's eldest soon will soon want to take the throne. Once he takes the throne, we are not queens anymore. We will just be princesses. His wife, or wives, will be the new queens. I hope that there is no rivalry that will emerge between us.'
'Mauro will be in charge as long as he is alive. So, his son has to wait for a while.'
'Ahh… there is the ship!'
'Where?'
'There!'
Huyên pointed on the horizon, where a small ship emerged to the surface.
'Finally!'
'He will land on the pier within ten minutes.'
'That is good!'
Huyên was correct. Within four minutes, the ship landed at the port. Some people got out, including a black couple. The couple was dressed in fine, French clothes. The man wore midnight blue and the wife light blue. The couple approached Maduro and Mauro. Mauro hinted towards his wives to come near.
'Come, Fiona!'
'I am coming!'
Both wives stood each one one side of Mauro and they held him by each putting one of their arms around him. The couple came closer, and they stopped at some point. Maduro came closer and the man handed a piece of paper to Maduro.
'This is the evidence that I would provide. It is me, Dean Jules! In person!'
'Good to have you here, Mister Jules. Good to have you here too, Mrs. Jules. Mister Oguntade is right over there with his two wives.'
'Two wives?'
'He has seven… those are his two recent ones.'
'A Spanish bride and an Asian one…'
'All his others are from our own people. Go and meet them!'
The couple then stood before Mauro and his two wives.
'Welcome to the Guatemala, Mister Jules! I am glad you took the effort to come all the way here!'
'It has been a long journey. Five weeks. I am finally here.'

'One of Spain's must peaceful kingdoms, bordering the Pacific Ocean and the Caribbean Sea.'
'Also, this is the sub-continent... or the bridge, between North and South America.'
'Correct... with a population of around 800.000 people... roughly. This place is quite at ease.'
'I see you brought your two treasures with you!'
'This on my right is Ifede, and the one on my left is Fayola.'
'Ifede, Fayola. This is my wife, Juliette.'
Juliette and Fiona made eye-contact. They recognised each other instantly.
'Nice to meet you, Mrs. Jules.'
'Nice to meet you to, Mrs. Oguntade. You too, Mrs. Oguntade!'
'So, let us go to San Pedro Sula to discuss business, shall we?'
'We will do!'
When the group arrived in San Pedro Sula, Dean rented a private room in one of the guesthouses. While Dean arranged an accommodation for him and his wife, the two childhood friends stood next to each other.
'So, Fiona...'
'Well, they call me Fayola here.'
'Well, Fayola... I never expected you to become a Zambo consort anytime soon.'
'Neither did I!'
'I am glad you are all right. It was a surprise to see you here!'
'Me too! The last time we saw each other was around a decade ago!'
'A lot changed since then.'
'We are grown women now.'
'Married also. Do you have children.'
'One daughter, Gabrielle. Her father is not Mauro.'
'You divorced?'
'It is kind of complicated.'
'What is not complicated in this world?'
'I met this man, in Matagalpa...'
'Where is Matagalpa?'
'It is this small district in the Province of Nicaragua.'
'Got it!'
'We got together, we have some good sex... and I became pregnant. He stayed with me during the pregnancy. However, just a week after our daughter was born... he left. Just like that. Suddenly, he came back, and

he told me that he could not bare to be with me due to the political afflictions of my family.'
'What a loser!'
'Indeed! I am glad I can keep him safely at a distance.'
'Do you remember that one teacher, who thought us Latin?'
'Yeah… Giorgio was his name, I believe.'
'Indeed!'
'What about him?'
'I heard that he was hung, in Sardinia.'
'What for?'
'He conspired to overthrow some mayor. He was sentenced to death.'
'When was this?'
'Two years ago.'
'Dang… that is harsh.'
'Do you have contact any of our former classmates?'
'I do not… well, with you now.'
'I used to hate it over there… however, after we returned to England, I continued to speak Spanish. I had to get used to English.'
'You moved to France.'
'I met Dean during one of his trips to London. We knew from that point on that we were a match!'
'Well, I met Mauro when he came to the Santa Barbara Foundation in Guatemala City to donate to some Mayan villages. He fancies me… and I surrendered.'
'You know how to recognise a stable man.'
'I learned from my mistake with my ex-fiancée.'
'That is good. We do not live thousands of years to make hundreds of mistakes. No mistake can be undone… only some consequences can be reversed. Even then, some mistakes you do not survive… so, it is good that we learn from human history.'
'Well, is there something to learn from history. It feels as if we are going in cycles.'
'That is what Dean is saying… history is like a loop, and later generations repeat the loop without knowing it.'
'If that is true… then the Spanish Empire will soon face its end… it is almost three centuries that Spain dominated the Western Hemisphere and around two centuries that Spain has been dominating the world's economy.'
'Well, we will see what happens.'

'I hope it does not happen during my lifetime though... I am a proud Spanish girl.'
'I am glad you are... Dean and I were thinking about leaving France. Due to the riots in Saint-Dominigue, we have received negative remarks from white French people on the streets. Things are getting out of hand there.'
'What about this Italian-born general, Napoleon... that took over?'
'That freak? Nobody likes him. However, because he has a more manly appearance, people think he has something to offer.'
'Does he?'
'I do not know... and I do not care. I just want me and Dean to be better off.'
'You think about moving to Spanish America?'
'Maybe... we were thinking of moving to Saint-Domingue. However, we do not know if François-Dominique Toussaint Louverture intends to declare independence or not. I have no interest in living in a Republic of Saint-Dominigue, if such a thing would ever exist.'
'Maybe he will change the name of the island after independence.'
'Again, we do not know what he will do.'
'In that case, you can always stay in Guatemala.'
'Yeah... that is another option. This place is more 'hidden' in the Western Hemisphere. So, there are pirates here... but you can easily hide from all the drama in the world.'
'I will be glad to have you here.'
'I need to discuss it with Dean. He might want to go back to France if we do not find a good settlement here.'
'You can live in Guatemala City or San Salvador. Those are quite modern cities here. Quetzaltenango is also a nice place.'
'What about the cities in the south?'
'Nicaragua and Costa Rica have smaller cities. However, the people are friendly over there... however, there are rival cities who still oppose Spanish rule, so you have to watch out with them.'
'Hmmm... good to know.'
'The closer to come to Mexico City, the better the cities are. The further away you go, the more crappy some of the places are. For example, Cartago, the capital of Costa Rica, is known as 'mud town' due to the bad sewers and ill-maintenance of its roads.'
'That is an embarrassment, especially for the capital of a Spanish province.'

‘It surely is… Guatemala City, San Salvador and San Pedro Sula, however, are top quality cities.’
‘I may request Dean to stay here for a while.’
‘How long did you intent to stay?’
‘Just a month.’
‘Stay longer!’
‘Yeah… that is my desire too.’
‘We can visit Costa Rica together… the Bocas del Toro bay is amazing!’
‘I am curious!’
While they still spoke, Dean came, and he kissed his wife.
‘It is settled!’
‘Great! Honey, I was talking to Fayola… we know each other from grammar school.’
‘What?’
‘Yeah… my parents put me in that school for two years when they were stationed in Guayaquil. There is where we met.’
‘Interesting!’
‘Anyway, can we stay longer in Guatemala?’
‘We can stay two months extra, that is three months in total.’
‘Great, then we can travel around.’
‘I was talking to Mauro… we can visit Lake Nicaragua soon. It is the biggest like of Central America as well as the Caribbean.’
‘Great!’
Fiona walked away. She arrived at a small tavern where she ordered a pancake with some strong coffee. While eating her dinner, she looked around her. There were youngsters that were talking about the weather, about girls and about their struggles in life. Inside, there was a map of Central America and there was a picture of King Charles IV and a picture of Crown-Prince Ferdinand, the Prince of Asturias. She checked the picture of her head of state and the heir to the throne. After eating her dinner, she saw Huyên entering the tavern.
‘Hey, here you are!’
‘You got some dinner!’
‘Just some little snacks. Mauro is looking for an accommodation for us here.’
‘Why do we not go to the village?’

‘It is a bit dangerous on the road at this time… and there is rain coming soon. Roads with rainwater on them are dangerous. Even if it’s a Spanish highway.’
‘I agree with that!’
‘Is that King Charles?’
‘Yeah’, Fiona pointed to the picture on the right, ‘that is him.’
‘He looks handsome.’
‘The left is our future king, Ferdinand VII when he takes over.’
‘Hmm… I heard that a lot of people have issues with Charles. He is not as ‘manly’ nor ‘active’ as people expect him to be.’
‘Ah… I receive such news too. Pedro Cevallos Guerra, our current Prime Minister, is the target of criminal conspiracies.’
‘Criminal conspiracies?’
‘Yeah… some criminals want to assassinate him because he shut down a smuggling route for Moroccan criminals.’
‘Ah…’
‘Several years ago, Malaspina was imprisoned for allegedly wanted to overthrow the Spanish government. His partner, José de Bustamante, was left out of the charges.’
‘Hmm… I do not know who that Malaspina is… but I did hear about Bustamante. Was he not captured by a British captain several years ago?’
‘Correct.’
‘He became famous…’
‘Just like one of our former Prime Ministers, Manuel Godoy y Álvarez de Faria.’
‘Is he not known as the *Prince of Peace*?’
‘Yes… I hate it that they gave him that tile. It is a type of blasphemy: only Christ is ever called the Prince of Peace in the Bible.’
‘Indeed… it is a type of idolatry!’
While they spoke, the bartender – a guy in his mid-thirties – handed them some papaya juice.
‘Ladies, I heard you spoke about the Prince of Peace?’
‘Oh… we were just discussing some of our Prime Ministers.’
‘Well, I was always a fun of Prime Minister Godoy. However, he had some weird attitude when it came to the Louisiana Territory.’
‘That place is being sold to France, right?’

'Well, that is the problem... Godoy arranged a take-over of the Province by France. However, France does not want to deal with those roaming Black men on horses...'
'Ah...'
'So, he kind of pushed the French to take it back... later Prime Ministers could not fully agree on the matter. However, it appears that within a year or two, the United States will take over Louisiana.'
'Wait...'
'That is the rumours.'
'If the United States takes over Louisiana, then that means that the United States will double in size overnight.'
'Correct.'
'That means that soon the United States will become a local power over here.'
'Maybe not... maybe they will. We just have to see.'
'Have you ever visited Spain?'
'Thrice... One time as a child.'
'When was that first time?'
'Somewhere in 1793... it was a very peaceful time back then. I have to tell you, some of the Spanish American cities are better looking than the actual Spanish cities in Spain.'
'What makes their cities worse off...'
'Not all of them... but... in Spain its mainly the capitals of the kingdoms are that good. The other cities are a bit neglected. That is why there is a lot of urban crime.'
'Ahh...'
'Under Charles III there were some improvements done to reduce urban crime. However, Charles IV, the current man we have... is not completing the job that his father began.'
'Which should be?'
'Banning foreign criminals all together and strengthening the Spanish unity. We need some event to unify people on the Iberian Peninsula. That will also benefit us here in New Spain.'
'It is funny you mention Guatemala as part of New Spain, many Guatemalans hate that.'
'I know... I am not the standard Guatemalan you will find. We are part of a viceroyalty and that is something to be proud of.'
'Indeed. I mean, the Viceroyalty of New Spain is the best one of all...'

‘It is the one with the most money also. The Viceroyalty of Peru is going bankrupt, and the Viceroyalty of New Granada has a growing Black population that is likely to revolt anytime soon.’
‘Ohh….’
‘Blacks are threated worse down there in South America than here in Central America. The only place, as far as I know, that Blacks have to themselves is Free Town Palenque and the Dutch colonies.’
‘The Dutch colonies?’
‘Black folks are not treated well anywhere in South America, but from what I understand, Black folks in the Dutch colonies have some leverage over the colonisers.’
‘That is interesting…’
‘The blacks I like the most are the French speaking ones from Saint-Dominigue. They are kicking the ass of the French. I am happy with that.’
‘Do you think Saint-Dominigue will become independent?’
‘If it does… it is good news. Then we have a wealthy, black island-nation that we can trade with. I prefer to trade with Blacks than to trade with whites… whites tend to rely too much on their governments and their governments, all in Europe, does not care about them.’
‘You are correct, my father is a nobleman in South America. He has been begging the Spanish government to invest more in the local infrastructure. Nothing has come from it. When he wanted to make effort on his own, he was stopped by the judge.’
‘What did he want to do?’
‘He wanted to dig a canal from his estate to a nearest river… so he could trade more freely.’
‘We sold him out?’
‘I think is one of my uncles…’
‘Ahh…’
‘My oldest uncle, who is the head of our family, wants to keep all the focus on the Iberian Peninsula, while my father wants more of the attention to go to South America.’
‘That might lead to more conflict in the future. I have relatives that lived in South America. Many of the criollos over there are upset that Spain remains the central focus of all the policies. They feel neglected.’
‘That is not good news…’

'On the other hand, South America does not bring that much revenue for the Spanish Crown anymore. Most of the income comes from New Spain and the Chinese trade in The Philippines.'
'Ah…'
'That means that Peru and Chile have become less relevant for the Spanish economy.'
'Got it!'
'So, in short… it is preferable for the Spanish Prime Ministers as well as the diplomats to invest more in their possessions in North America, Asia and the Caribbean… than to invest in South America. South America has a growing population, but there is also growing concerns. The bigger the population becomes; the more people want to live in big cities. The more people live in big cities, the less people there are on the farms. The less people on the farms, less food for the locals and less export… the less export, more economic difficulties.'
'So, in the future we might see a lot of civil unrest in South America?'
'Exactly! IF there was a place that might become independent soon, it is likely to be Peru or New Granada. I do not see that going well for long.'
'I was thinking to move to Buenos Aires sometime when I am older. It is the most 'Spanish' place there is outside of Spain, I heard. I visited it twice when I was younger. Once at eleven and three years later, at age fourteen.'
'I never had the chance to visit Buenos Aires, but I would love to in the future. But there is one thing I figured out about our Spanish Empire that many do not realise… this empire is not going to last that long anymore. At least, not in South America. South America has too many challenges for the Spanish government.'
'Do you think independence will be a good idea?'
'Absolutely not… but… with the demographic and infrastructural challenges ahead, there is no doubt that soon… some opportunistic fool will take advantage to establish their own countries.'
'That would be a fun thing to experience.'
'Well, not if you are living there!'
'We live in Guatemala, far away from all those issues.'
While they spoke, Mauro entered in.
'Hey!'
Both wives kissed him. The bartender offered Mauro some juice. He declined.
'It was nice talking! See ya!'

'See ya!'
Outside, Mauro informed them that he found an accommodation for them. It is a three room flat with their own balcony and their own bath.
'That is great!'
'We have it for at least a month.'
'A month?'
'Yes... we will go to the village... but we will have to entertain our guests as long as they are in our country.'
'Sure!'
'Come... we need to go home!'
The three arrived in the flat and Fiona was excited when she saw how beautifully decorated the place was. Fiona received the room with a view on the mountains. She was happy with it. Her room even had a tiny balcony where she could sit in. However, she had no interest of opening nay windows or doors when night fell. Nights could be chilly in Central America.
When she sat in her room, she looked in the mirror. She longed to put on some of her Spanish dresses. The next day, she purchased three new dresses, and some shoes, in town. She paid with two Spanish Escudos (minted in Spain, three years earlier).
That evening, after dinner, she took a warm shower and she then went on putting on one of the dresses in her room. She put on two earrings, with sun-shaped decorations in them (consisting out of tiny jewels). She had three bracelets on her right arm which she purchased in Guatemala City months before. Her dress was light yellow, and she wore a light-yellow top beneath it. She was glad about her new outfit. She added yellow sandals to finish the decoration. While she was standing in front of the mirror, someone knocked on the door.
'Come in!'
Nobody answered.
'Come in!'
Nobody answered.
She walked to the door and opened it. She looked around the corner. She was smiling, still euphoric about her new dress. Her euphoria blinded her from sensing that the situation was off.
'Anyone there?'
The doorknob had a flower painting surrounding it.
She left her room and she walked through the flat. When she arrived in the living room, she saw Mauro and Huyên mating loudly. She walked

back without disturbing them. When she was back at the door of her room, she saw that the window on the hallway was open.
'Who opened that?'
She walked towards the window and she saw that there was a piece of textile that was torn at the window. She looked down from the window and she saw a footprint in the sand.
'What is this?'
She walked back to her room and she closed the door. After several minutes, she even locked it to be sure. She decided to sit in her balcony. The view on the mountains was great. From her window, she began to play on the baroque guitar that was there in the balcony. She played several Spanish songs, and she sang along with it. She loved singing. She checked the Spanish flag, on the outside wall of their flat, while remembering her time at the Foundation.
After singing her fifth song, she became thirsty. She went back inside and by now Mauro and Huyên were dressed.
'I will be back soon!'
Mauro left.
'You have a beautiful voice.'
'Thanks, Huyên!'
'You should sing more often.'
'I was thinking about that too...'
'Mauro delighted in it!'
'While he was bouncing into you.'
'Yeah…'
'Huyên… did you hear someone upstairs?'
'I was distracted, you know… with a handsome man as Mauro inside of you…'
'I mean it… did you hear something, even afterwards?'
'No…'
'Come with me!'
Huyên went upstairs with Fiona. She pointed towards the window and the torn-off textile.
'This looks like a piece of a shirt that has been torn when someone left via the window.'
'That is what I was thinking. Someone knocked on my door. I said to come in… the individual did not come in. So, I went to check, and I saw nobody. But then… I noticed the window and this.'
'This is creepy!'

'It is for sure!'
'Let us check your room.'
'All right!'
When the two entered her room, they got cold chills.
'The door to your balcony is closed…'
'And there is no cold weather outside.'
'What the hell?'
The women checked the room to see if anything was out of line. Then, Huyên got the idea to look beneath the bed.
'Fiona… check beneath the bed. You are the leanest of us two… and you are not pregnant.'
'True… hold on!'
Fiona put off her sandals, her dress, and her earrings. She was only left with her top and bracelets. While checking the floor beneath, she found a key. She grabbed it and she showed it to Huyên.
'What is that key for?'
'I have no idea… do we have something like a basement or some wardrobe?'
'We can go downstairs to check it out.'
The two women went downstairs, and they entered the kitchen. While walking around, Fiona noticed that there was some looseness beneath one of the small carpets.
'Hold this… Huyên!'
Fiona removed the small carpet, and she found a hatch in the floor.
'Hmm… what is that?'
'Huyên… we are about to find out!'
Fiona used the key and the hatch opened.
'What is down there?'
There was a weird stench that came to them. Fiona lit on an oil lamp and she walked downstairs. When she was down, she saw shelves with glass pots. The pots contained spices and conserved foot. When, however, she saw it.
There was a skeleton down there… with some clothes on it.
'Huyên… there is a corpse down here!'
'What?'
'There is a skeleton… to be more precise… whoever it is. He, I think it is a he… has been death for a while.'
'What type of clothes are it?'

‘I see a medal on his chest… I think he was some type of sailor or something.’
‘Take the medal and come up!’
She did that and she closed the hatch after being back up.
‘Put back the carpet…’
Fiona listened. Both women then checked the medal.
‘This medal… is made somewhere in 1787.’
‘That is almost fourteen years… thirteen now.’
‘It is a bronze medal for participating in a military conflict. It is often rewarded to veterans who were injured during warfare.’
‘Look at the back?’

Santiago Hernandez y Cobán,
1st Infantry of the Kingdom of Guatemala.

‘Hmm… in late 1780s, there was a big conflict with the British due to Spanish support for the independent of the United States. There was even a moment that the British landed in Honduras and occupied it for a few days.’
‘Hmmm….’
‘This soldier likely fought during that war.’
‘However, how did he end up here?’
‘Someone must have been missing him!’
‘They should… we at least know his name. Santiago.’
‘There are so many men named Santiago, both Portuguese and Spanish ones.’
‘We know his two last names. That should be enough to look up his relatives.’
‘Do they want to know about him? That is what I am wondering.’
‘What do you mean?’
‘A war hero like him… and nobody misses him?’
‘Hmm… maybe he was killed after being honoured.’
‘He might have died down where when the shaft closed in on him.’
‘This shaft is not that powerful… with all the heavy bottles down there and even some of the metal pins, he could have broken out easily.’
‘That means that he was likely knocked out… and then placed there and the hatch was locked above him.’
‘This is homicide.’
‘Dang…’

Huyên went to the living room to sit down. Fiona remained in the kitchen to check things around. She found a small document, hidden behind one of the shelves. She went with the document to Huyên.
'What is that?'
'Likely something related to that murdered soldier.'
'Hmmm….'
Fiona opened the document and she saw that it was receipts of payment he received from the military. The last one was dated 1st of October 1788. The payment consisted out of 220 Spanish Real.[35]
'It states here that he was born in León, Province of Nicaragua, on the 15th of September 1761. So, he was twenty-seven when he received his last payment.'
'And he vanished…'
'What should we do with this.'
'We have to inform the authorities about it.'
'It has been more than a decade now.'
'They can still reach out to the relatives. They may still be able to give him a proper burial.'
'That is a good idea.'
'Stay here!'
Fiona left the house and she walked towards the house of the mayor. The mayor, however, had a guard that protected his place. She asked one of the guards to call the mayor. The mayor came.
'What can I do for you, ma'am.'
'Sir, I am Fiona Rodrigues. I am lodging in your beautiful city for a month. I was visiting a friend of mine and we found this hatch in the floor. There is a corpse beneath it.'
'Oh, Holy Mary!'
'We found some documents in the kitchen too. They were hidden… the remains belong to this soldier, likely.'
She handed the documents to the mayor. The mayor checked them.
'Good that you shown us this. Please, keep this with you… tomorrow a team will come to investigate.'
'Please send them now. The couple is not comfortable with a decade old corpse beneath their kitchen!'
'You are right!'
The mayor called in some officers and he ordered them to go to the rented flat to do their investigation.

---

[35] In today's money €1.402,50

Around midnight, the corpse was removed from the kitchen and the documents were taken as evidence.
'What will happen with the corpse?'
'He will receive a burial in León. His family will be informed coming days. It is a shame that he ended up this way. Since the crime happened more than a decade ago, and because this property changed hands multiple times, we might never figure out what happened to him. At least, his relatives will have peace now.'
'That is what I am happy about!'
The officers left. Huyên and Mauro were perplexed.
'What is going on?'
'You were quite sharp, Fayola!'
'I know Maawiya… I am not always distracted, hahaha.'
'Well, Ifede told me about what you experienced… that knocking on the door.'
'Yeah… I forgot to tell you.'
'When I was out… people told me stories of this place.'
'What kind of stories.'
'After the war with Britain, around the independence of the United States, there was this old couple that lived here… Mayans. They were fighting all the time and their children and grandchildren did not want anything to do with them. One day, the old woman killed her husband and then committed suicide. For three years, the building remained vacant. Then there was this mestizo soldier that moved here. I believe his name was Santiago or Tiago. He had a wife and a little daughter. One day, the man comes home, and he finds out that his wife left him for some stranger. She took the daughter with them. He lost his mind and he attempted suicide by drowning himself in the nearest river. He recovered. Soon after that, the man just disappeared.'
'When did he disappear…'
'Somewhere after Christmas of 1788. Last month, a young lady and an older man came to this place. The property owner did not want to rent it to them… which was odd. There was a whole fight about it. Then two days before I rented it… someone tried to break in. The neighbours caught him, and he ran away.'
'Hmm…. he might have come back!'
'The man allegedly was looking for what belonged to his father.'
'Father?'
'He said his father lived there and he had not seen him for a while…'

‘Hmmm…. what could Santiago have kept hidden here?’
‘That guitar upstairs… Fayola. That might have been Santiago’s.’
‘Hmm… he knocked on my door… whoever broke in. So, maybe there is something hidden in my room. Maawiya, come and look with me.’
‘I am coming.’
After an hour of looking around, Mauro found a hole in the wall. When he checked it better, he realised that there was a little wardrobe that was painted over.
‘Fayola… there is a wardrobe here.’
‘Open it!’
He opened it…
‘Oh Gosh…’
‘That is a lot of money!’
‘How much do you think it is?’
‘To my guess… with all those Escudo coins and all those Spanish Dollars… at least a half million Real worth of cash.’
‘A half million! This is a fortune!’
‘Hmm… if Santiago had a son before he met his wife, that son might be the one looking for this.’
‘We need to check who that son is and hand it over to him. It is rightfully his.’
‘We will do… let us hope he is still alive. My gut feeling is telling me that this soldier did not earn this money the right way. That might explain how he was found in kitchen’s basement.’
‘I have to admit… you are right about this one.’
‘Hold on…’
‘What is it?’
‘Look!’
Mauro showed a painting with the name of the soldier written below.
‘A self-portrait.’
‘He was a handsome man.’
‘He surely was… such a waste!’
‘It is important to know who you hang around. I have the feeling that this young man got involved with the wrong people, during his military career and that this is how he ended up like this. During the civil war in what would later become the United States, many Spanish soldiers got involved with money changers as well as pirates. This might have been one of such cases.’
‘That might explain it.’

'In that case, us renting this place is a blessing for that young man. He will be a very wealthy man from now on.'
'We need to find him, and we need to coach him. There is no way that with this amount of money people will let him live.'
'Normally… you do not notice things that quickly. This time you are right on it!'
'Thanks, darling!'
They kissed one another.
'Darling?'
'Yeah?'
'It is time for me to get some of your affection…'
She closed the wardrobe and dragged Mauro with her, on the blankets…

Lightning Source UK Ltd.
Milton Keynes UK
UKHW010644280521
384539UK00002B/228